# *The vidscreen blazed with destruction now.*

They had shifted into the solar system at the beginning of the vicious self-extermination games. Norlin hoped the emperor went blind watching such good men and women slaughtered at his whim.

He worked to get the *Preceptor* inward of Saturn's orbit and to the space station circling Earth. Carefully avoiding the larger ships, he corkscrewed over and under the asteroids and thought he had made the perilous journey unscathed when alarms flashed up and down his board.

"Midget battleship detected," barked out Chikako Miza. "Closing fast."

"Full defensives out. They pushed our ECM missile array aside. We're using lasartillery to the fullest. We're beginning to overload. They're throwing everything at us. We're their only target." Sarov's dour voice carried a load of gloom with it. Norlin saw why as he studied the readouts dashing in front of his face. The heads-up display gave him only the highlights of his officers' reports.

He went cold inside when the ship's sensors picked up the visual on the midget battleship.

"That's Emperor Arian's personal ship," he muttered. "We're facing the best ship in the whole damned Empire Service fleet!"

ALSO BY
*Robert E. Vardeman*

**STAR FRONTIERS**

*Alien Death Fleet*
*The Genetic Menace*

**AFTER THE SPELL WARS**

*Ogre Castle*
*In The Sea Nymph's Lair*

STAR FRONTIERS BOOK 3

# THE BLACK
# NEBULA

# ROBERT E.
# VARDEMAN

ZUMAYA OTHERWORLDS                    AUSTIN TX

2014

This book is a work of fiction. Names, characters, places and incidents are products of the author's imagination or are used fictitiously. Any resemblance to actual persons or events is purely coincidental.

THE BLACK NEBULA

© 2015 by Robert E. Vardeman

ISBN 978-1-934841-94-5

Cover art © Brad W. Foster

Cover design © Tamian Wood

"Zumaya Otherworlds" and the griffon colophon are trademarks of Zumaya Publications LLC, Austin TX.

Look for us online at http://www.zumayapublications.com

Library of Congress Cataloging-in-Publication Data

Vardeman, Robert E.
  The black nebula / Robert E. Vardeman.
     pages cm. — (Star frontiers ; 3)
   ISBN 978-1-934841-94-5 (print/trade pbk. : alk. paper) — ISBN 978-1-934841-95-2 (electronic/multiple format : alk. paper) (print) — ISBN 978-1-61271-103-4 (electronic/epub : alk. paper) (print)
  1. Space ships—Fiction. I. Title.
  PS3572.A714B57 2012
  813'.54—dc23
                              2012037662

# Chapter One

The spider-like alien cowered in the corner of his prison cell. Taloned fingers tentatively dragged along the composite material wall, exploring for any small hope of escape. Try as he might, the Kindarian could not scratch the tough material. The stainless steel bars welded over the doorway effectively kept him from overpowering the peculiarly shaped human guard and escaping.

He hunkered down even more and hunched his back, trying to return to the primal-egg position. Never had such shame been heaped upon him. Captured by the enemy! Worse, they had gathered important information from him. Why had he spoken to the lumpy human of the racial home world? He had taken a solemn vow on his spawning web to die before revealing such information.

His compound eyes blurred, the closest he could come to imitating human tears. Frustration and anger mounted. He had betrayed his own kind. He had spoken of the Black Nebula. He had provided coordinates even these curiously autonomous humans could decipher. The only thing he had not spoken of was the Fountain of Spacefaring. If they had asked about this, he would have killed himself to prevent speaking of his race's most holy shrine.

Talons scratched at the wall again. Not even a tiny sliver of the tough material came free. Eyes darting up, he waited for the guard to pass outside. A food tray was shoved under the welded bars for him. He took it to give the illusion of continued cooperation.

Only when he was certain the guard had left, not wanting to endure watching him eat, did he move to the back of the cell. The spot on the wall he had chosen suited him well enough; he had no way of telling what lay in the next compartment. Human spaceships were designed with a half-witted maze of corridors that confused his logical mind and wasted space. They lacked the proper web-shaped interior construction prevalent on all Kindarian battle craft.

He spat some of his digestive juices onto the wall. Using his talon, he concentrated it within a small circle. In seconds, the composite wall bubbled and began to turn tacky. He pushed gently, causing the material to bulge outward. He spat stomach acid in a hosing gush.

Paranoia caused him to pause when noise came from the corridor. A robot repair unit passed by, oblivious to his activity. The guard had not returned to collect his food tray and based on previous feedings would not for hours. He worked faster. His body produced stomach fluid twice a day; he had only a few more minutes of his digestive phase before the glands stopped making the caustic fluid. He would go hungry until the evening feeding—or what he construed as evening.

He could endure. He was a Kindarian warrior. He should have died for his race and hadn't. It was time to redeem himself and perform a noble task worthy of the First Hatchling. He had to strike out against the enemy.

The digestive acid hissed and popped and eventually cut through the carbon composite wall. Sharp talons dug at the edges, hurrying the process. When the hole was only fifty centimeters in diameter, he ran out of digestive juice.

The hole was large enough, although no watching human would have believed it possible for the chitinous body to fit. Getting all eight limbs through proved the work of a second. His heavy thorax was more difficult, but he twisted and wiggled and succeeded.

Escape! This did not seem to be another cell. For long minutes, he stood in darkness in the next compartment, trying to decipher the peculiar odors, and hearing sounds beyond his understanding.

He moved into the room and decided the soft, rhythmic sighing came from a sleeping human. Wiggling the antennae just above his eyes, he picked up a new smell—a scent of aberration.

He almost bolted and ran. He had entered the sleeping web of the human afflicted with madness! Why did they permit such defective units in their midst? No Kindarian would tolerate such deviant behavior in another.

He was a warrior of the Third Web, second hatching, highest elevation. He had been destined to greatness from the egg. It was his duty to kill all who violated the law of the web.

As he stood over the sleeping human, the one they called Gowan Liottey, a taloned hand reached out and lightly touched the burning-hot human's cheek. The talon's sharp edge moved lower to rest against an exposed, pulsing artery. A single slash of that deadly talon would end this miserable one's life.

But the warrior held back. This was the *Preceptor*'s second-in-command, who would replace their demon captain if he were to die. To kill the one seized with madness was to defeat his own goals, he realized after a moment's reflection.

Kill the capable human captain, and this one, this defective officer, would assume command. He clacked his razor-edged mandibles at the thought and rubbed his antennae together with the first twinge of joy he had felt since being ripped from his scout ship. His plan to kill their captain and elevate this one in his stead was audacious and might redeem him in the heart of the Supreme.

"What the hell's going on in here? Alarms are ringing all over the damned ship."

Lights flared and blinded the Kindarian. He threw up a protecting limb and spun to face the door. The guard had discovered him!

"Move, soft one, and I will slice this one's throat," he croaked in his best imitation of human speech. The talon rested against Gowan Liottey's throat.

Only then did the sleeping first officer awaken. His blue eyes went wide, and he started to scream.

"Stay calm, Gowan," the one called Tia Barse cautioned. "The bug got out of his cell." Her gaze darted to the wall adjoining the infirmary and found the hole. "He chewed through, somehow. He's not going to hurt you, or he would have done it by now."

"Wrong," the Kindarian cried. "I will slay without mercy."

"Do it, and you die on the spot," Barse snapped. She drew her laser pistol and aimed it at the alien.

He prepared to die, but he would take the recumbent Liottey with him. The talon pressed down and a bead of blood form on the man's throat.

"No, Barse, don't let him!" Liottey whined.

"This is for the best, Gowan," taunted Barse. She moved to get a better shot at the alien.

The Kindarian knew he was faster and had heard them comment on how spindly he looked. He was far stronger than any of the humans. She would try to cut off the strongest of his legs to keep him from attacking her. He shifted his carapace to make this difficult without risking that the shot would damage Liottey.

"Ever since you sniffed that CoolinGas, you've been one royal pain in the butt."

"Tia!" pleaded Liottey. "Don't! I—"

"You're whining, Gowan. Stop it." She took careful aim.

The Kindarian moved his talon slightly, to producing a red trickle down the first officer's throat. A fraction of a millimeter more, and the carotid artery would be severed.

"Don't sweat it, Gowan. The auto-med unit will repair the wound quickly enough if I have to shoot the bug. He's smart enough to avoid me shooting him. He's going to crawl back into his cage and not harm you."

Eyes flashing and antennae restless, the Kindarian tried to estimate what value Liottey actually had. From scent and body set, the female had no respect for the hostage human's abilities. He tried to integrate his other senses. The female had an active hatred for the male.

4

The Kindarian reformed his plans. If he killed the human captain to install the one under his talon, the female might slay Liottey without a qualm.

Still, Tia Barse hesitated. The Kindarian understood the reason. He was the enemy, the alien. Even one spurned from the web ranked higher than any from another race.

"I saw the telltales going red," came a deep, resonant voice. "When I couldn't pick it up on vidscreen I came down. What's going on?" Pier Norlin froze when he saw the tableau in front of him.

This complicated matters. To die without slaying the human captain meant added failure and disgrace. To kill a mere secondary officer of lesser value accomplished nothing.

"I'll burn the bug, Cap'n," Barse promised. "The auto-med unit can fix up Liottey."

"Wait." Norlin touched a stud on the com-link at his belt. "Don't do anything." He spoke directly to the Kindarian to stay the talon on his second officer's throat. The Kindarian appreciated the acceptance of his rank, but he worried the demon captain only sought delay.

"Stay calm. What do you want?"

"Want?" This took him by surprise. He had not thought the captain of such a mighty ship would deign to negotiate. Humans continued to present him with unsettling puzzles. How could Pier Norlin face a significant element of the Kindarian Death Fleet and win, yet be willing to discuss the life of a single, lesser warrior? Especially an incompetent one such as Gowan Liottey?

The scents emitted by both of the other humans almost overwhelmed him with contempt—for their own crew member. He needed time to decide if this was a sensory mask cast by the humans to hide their true intentions and attacks. If only the Supreme had discovered more of their evolutionary path to better understand motivations, but until now, there had been no need. The Death Fleet crept past their crude sensors, destroyed what planetary defenses existed, looted the planet and moved on.

What need was there to understand such primitives?

"You think to trick me."

"No," said Norlin. "Barse, clear out. Get back to engineering."

"I can burn the bug, Cap'n. I *can!*"

"That's an order, Lieutenant. Shift out of here, now!"

The power struggle confused him. The female resisted an order from her superior. How was that possible? How was it not met with instant punishment? Perhaps he held a stronger tactical position than he thought, and this captain was not truly in command. As strange as it seemed, he might kill Liottey but in doing so remove the only bargaining wedge he had.

Barse grumbled and left, her pistol still centered on the Kindarian's thorax all the way out of the infirmary.

When she had gone, Norlin said, "Don't do anything hasty. Just stay calm." He backed away and left. The door slid shut, leaving the warrior with his talon pressed into the terrified Liottey's throat.

He was more perplexed than ever at their actions. The humans had simply…retreated. This made no sense.

He settled down to wait. Time rode heavily on him as he worked over the probabilities of success in his mind. The numbers shifted constantly and left him uncertain.

He hated that.

✳ ✳ ✳

"No loss," grumbled the tactical officer. Mitri Sarov swiveled back and forth in his chair, his powerful hands clenching and unclenching as if he had the brittle-appearing Kindarian's throat in his grip. The feathery scars forming a faint web under his left eye pulsed with a pink inner glow. "Liottey never amounted to more than a red dwarf—lots of gas and no heat."

"He's an officer in this crew," Norlin said somberly. "As such, we must try to save him. I agree he's not the best officer in the Empire Service, but he belongs to us, to the *Preceptor.*"

"Dammit," muttered the communications officer, Chikako Miza. The shaved sides of her head gleamed in the bright light of the control room. Her tall, dark, woven topknot shimmered with the com gear she had woven through it.

A vague expression crossed her face; then, the usual sharpness returned. Norlin wondered what tidbit of information had flashed through her com. When she didn't offer to tell him, he ignored it. Everyone aboard the *Preceptor* had pressing work to do that didn't reflect directly on their immediate problem.

"We rescue him…how?"

"Gas," came Tia Barse's voice over the com-link to the engine room. The engineer had retreated there and labored to keep the equipment functioning at peak.

"I can talk to him," spoke up Trahnee.

"Not yet," Norlin said to the dark-haired, grey-eyed woman. Trahnee was genhanced and controlled others with the subsonic pitching of her voice. Only she had been able to interrogate the prisoner properly; only she had worked out the coordinates of the Black Nebula from the alien's vague descriptions of star pattern.

"Why not? I turn on the intercom and speak to him. It is that simple. Unless you want to forfeit Liottey, of course."

"Let her do it. If it doesn't work, we can try the narcotic gas, as Barse suggested," said Sarov. The man's thick fingers worked on the keyboard at his console. Norlin knew different scenarios for attacking the hostage problem had been set up, and the tactical officer computed the course of action with the greatest chance of success.

"Do it," he said, deciding. He pointed to the com-link at his belt. Trahnee reached out and took it. Norlin couldn't help himself—her nearness excited him. He felt a thrill just having her fingers brush across his stomach on their way to the com-link.

"There is no hope," she said softly into the unit, not prefacing it with a greeting to the Kindarian as she had always done before to focus his attention. "Surrender. We will not harm you if you surrender and leave Liottey uninjured. You cannot triumph. Surrender…surrender…surrender."

Norlin saw Sarov struggling under the genhanced power of that suggestion; the bulky tac officer wanted to give up. Chikako Miza turned up whatever she listened to in her earpiece to drown out the Lorelei's seductive voice. Norlin shivered and threw off the hypnotic spell of her voice—he was partially immune to her power. Why, he did not know or care to find out. The others succumbed with varying degrees of ease.

"It's not working, Cap'n," came Barse's voice in his head-phones. "The alien's got something stuffed into his ears, or what-ever he uses to hear. Might be, he catches vibrations against the cilia on those spiky antennas—he's got 'em all tucked up under his carapace, out of sight. He's a smart one. He's learned how she can twist him up inside, like she's done with you."

"Lieutenant!" Norlin snapped.

"It's not working on him," muttered Barse, not chastised in the least.

Sarov shook his head. Trahnee's voice had failed to carry the day.

"Never mind," said Norlin. "We hit him with the narco gas. Do it, Barse."

"Done, Cap'n." For several seconds the engineer said noth-ing. Then: "That didn't work, either. He's got an oxygen bottle rigged up and is using it. He expected us to gas him, the clever bastard."

"Get RRUs going on the outer hull," said Norlin. "Drill through. Evacuate the section."

"What? Why?" demanded Trahnee. "That will kill Liottey, too. You didn't want that."

"The *Preceptor* is at risk," Norlin said. "The Kindarian is in-dependent of our atmosphere, at least until the medical oxygen supply is exhausted. In that time, he can work up any number of explosive devices using the supplies in that compartment. I want to limit the time he has to think up such nastiness as well as keep him off balance worrying about the wrong things."

He turned and punched up a schematic of that portion of the *Preceptor* on the vidscreen. He used a small laser wand to point out the sections endangered if an internal explosion occurred.

"He can take out the main power line," said Trahnee. "That would require considerable explosive, though."

"He can do it with nothing more than the gases stored in the infirmary," said Chikako. "Mix and match them—boom!" She threw her hands up to indicate what could happen.

"Even if the alien did not attempt that," said Sarov, "the drugs and chemicals form a powerful arsenal. He can concoct explo-sives that will rip through our guts. I've closed blast doors fore and aft of the infirmary."

Norlin nodded. He had a good crew. They protected the ship well.

"You can't evacuate the infirmary. Liottey will die!" Trahnee protested.

"He's an officer in the Empire Service," said Sarov. "He knew he might die in combat."

"*You're* killing him," the woman protested.

Sarov's face went pale. His lower lip quivered.

"She's right," he said in an uncharacteristically shaky voice. "We can't do this."

For Sarov to act that way, she must have used her genetically enhanced persuasion. Norlin set the command wand to send shrill feedback into the tac officer's headphones. Sarov reacted instantly. He threw his hands up to his ears to jerk away the source of the offending noise but then left the 'phones in place. He shot an angry look at Trahnee and turned back to his board.

"Do not influence my crew in that way," Norlin ordered her softly. "We appreciate the gravity of the situation. You apparently do not. Saving Liottey is secondary to saving the *Preceptor*…and our own lives."

"Let me go reason with the Kindarian. He listened before. He'll do it again if I can just face him."

"Barse says he has blocked out your voice by hiding those antennae. In a real sense, he is totally deaf. We must capitalize on this weakness, especially if he thinks it is his strength dealing with us."

Norlin studied the progress of the robot repair units as they magnetically scampered along the hull to a spot just outside the infirmary. The reactive armor and heavy plating made drilling difficult—the *Preceptor* was a war vessel and designed to take substantial punishment before its hull was breached. The RRUs might have to work for ten minutes or longer to bore through and explosively decompress the sealed compartment.

"They're working, Cap'n," came the engineer's voice in his headphones. A sudden pop indicated Barse had switched to a private com frequency. "Do we really want to suck the bastard's lungs out like this?"

"We do. You know what we've stored in that chamber. The alien can seriously damage us if he uses a chemical bomb."

"Hell, he doesn't even have to blow stuff up. Cap'n—he could overload our atmospheric filtration unit, he could set a phosphorus fire that might burn for days, he could—"

"Keep the RRUs at work, Lieutenant."

"Aye, aye, Cap'n."

Norlin looked at Trahnee. The woman's stricken expression told of the stress on her. In that moment, he loved her even more.

He knew she didn't care for Liottey—none of them did—but she had taken his part and sought a way for him to live. No one in the infirmary was likely to survive.

"Got a glitch, Cap'n. RRU number two broke down."

"Keep the first unit working."

"Takes longer."

"Keep drilling," Norlin ordered. He cursed the lack of working vidscreen pickup in the infirmary. They had set alarms while Liottey was in there; the vidcams had been moved to more important locations. The *Preceptor* needed a complete refit. They had been through too many battles and had accumulated too many scars.

Norlin smiled grimly. That applied to his crew, too. And to him. Too many battles, too many scars, not enough R&R or time to heal.

"Picking up strange noises in the infirmary," said Chikako Miza. "Can't place, them. They're—"

"Status report," Norlin snapped, interrupting the com officer. "How long before the RRU makes it through?"

"Another ten minutes, Cap'n. Unit two is completely dead. Fused circuit, I think. Have to do a complete overhaul to be sure."

He cursed. The alien was up to something. The Kindarian had had eight minutes to fix the oxygen mask to his strange face then explore the cabinets and storage lockers in the infirmary. The alien was sufficiently advanced to know what a treasure trove of destructive capability it had blundered across.

Norlin knew he should have put the alien in a more secure compartment. Welding bars across the doorway had forced the Kindarian to seek other escape routes. How the alien had melted its way through the carbon composite wall was something that needed further study—if they managed to stop the escape without dying themselves.

"Noise level picking up."

Norlin checked the chronometer. Still more than nine minutes before the RRU bored through. He wished Trahnee had been successful or the narcotic gas had put the Kindarian to sleep. He felt the tension tightening his gut and sending his heart racing until he almost gasped for air. The *Preceptor* was at stake.

"It's Liottey," said Miza, her dark eyes widening in surprise. "He's overcome the sleepy gas Barse pumped in. He…he's going after the Kindarian!"

Norlin heard a bellow of rage that was scarcely human. A loud crash followed, and then came sounds of intense struggle.

"Barse, get into the infirmary. Take a laser rifle. Fry the alien. If Liottey gets in the way, too bad, but don't let it escape."

He grabbed a pistol from a rack by the door and tossed it to Trahnee as he rushed out. Norlin had no idea what was happening in the infirmary, but this might give them their chance to eliminate the alien and save Gowan Liottey.

Or doom them all.

# Chapter Two

**G**owan Liottey shrieked and blasted upward from his bed. Tubes sunk into his veins ripped free. Blood and healing solutions spewed across the infirmary. He never noticed. Probes taped to his body pulled over instruments fastened to a table beside his bed. He never felt the skin ripping slightly as the probes yanked free from his flesh.

The auto-med unit beeped a protest at such unseemly behavior from its patient then settled down to a constant one-note complaint.

Liottey heard and saw nothing but the Kindarian in front of him. The CoolinGas leak in the chamber where he had worked without a respirator had disrupted neural paths in his brain. Normally hesitant, Liottey's personality had changed to aggressive. He attacked the alien. His fingers raked like claws. He kicked and fought and ignored the alien's talons ripping and slashing his body.

Liottey's strong white teeth fastened on a spindly alien arm poking from beneath the creature's torso. Jaw muscles contracted and ripped open stiff body flesh. Liottey spat blood and chitin and kept attacking, bowling over the Kindarian with the sheer mindless fury of his attack.

"Cease, stop, I surrender!" the alien bellowed.

Liottey did not hear. His berserker rage knew no bounds. He grabbed the alien by the throat and jerked hard, trying to break the connection between thorax and head.

The Kindarian brought up four of his taloned hind walking limbs and tried to force the *Preceptor*'s first officer away. The effort failed. Liottey's insane strength kept the alien pinned to the deck and helpless.

"Gowan, stop!" came Norlin's sharp command. "You've beaten him. Stop. That's an order!"

Tia Barse joined Norlin in pulling the man off his victim. The Kindarian curled into an egg-shaped ball, shaking all over.

"Hold him," ordered Norlin. He thrust his laser pistol under the Kindarian's face. The spider-like being was defeated. He stopped fighting.

"The doctors never predicted such a reaction," murmured Trahnee from the doorway. She held her weapon clumsily, not wanting to use it. Norlin took it from her and trained it on the alien.

"Get up. We're putting you under constant surveillance. Barse, how's Liottey?"

"Collapsed. The burst of rage burned up his energy reserves. He's weak as a kitten now." The engineer turned when she heard a loud purring sound. Around her feet wove a black cat with gray stripes in its tail and a spattering of brown along its belly. Barse's nose wrinkled.

Norlin took an involuntary step away from the methane-producing cat.

"I told you not to feed Neutron so much protein. He stinks worse every time I see him."

"Flatulence can be used as a weapon," Barse said. "Let me lock the cat up with the bug. That would definitely constitute cruel and unusual punishment—and deserved, to my way of thinking."

She poked the Kindarian with the toe of her boot. The alien did not react. He had withdrawn completely into an ego-web and made no move to respond.

"My arms," moaned Liottey. "My body. What's wrong? Why do I hurt so much?"

Norlin went to his first officer's side and knelt.

"You just saved us a lot of trouble."

Norlin and Barse both looked up just as the RRU laser drill cut through the hull.

Sudden decompression resulted. Norlin grabbed Trahnee and shoved her into the corridor away from the turbulence blowing out through the hole in the wall. Barse and Liottey managed to join them in the corridor. Only the Kindarian remained in the infirmary, tightly balled like a larva.

"We forgot to turn off the drill," cried Norlin over the rush of air past him and through the infirmary. "Get the hatch closed."

"We'll kill the prisoner," protested Barse. "We *need* him. I've got to find out about the alien star drive engines. And that rainbow ray weapon. And—"

"Close the damned door." Norlin leaned past and cycled the infirmary door shut. The air loss continued. He cursed and went to the hatch to the Kindarian's cell. Air gushed through the hole the alien had cut. Norlin shut off this chamber, too.

"Get the RRU to work fixing the hull," he ordered Barse. "I want to reestablish pressure as quickly as possible. We might be able to save the Kindarian."

Trahnee spoke quietly to Liottey, reassuring him, quieting him. In minutes, the first officer slumped and snored loudly.

Trahnee looked up at Norlin.

"He will sleep until I order him to awaken. It is for his own good. He is exhausted."

"Did you get any idea out of him why he pinned the alien like he did? Liottey's never shown much in the way of courage before." Norlin snorted in contempt. The opposite was true. Gowan Liottey went out of his way to choose the path of least resistance—the course of maximum cowardice.

"The CoolinGas must have affected him in ways we didn't anticipate. The doctors planetside did what they could with cortical transplants. This might signal a permanent change in his personality."

"Courage we can use. Foolhardiness is a commodity we already have in abundance," Norlin said.

"Pressure's back, Cap'n," reported Barse. "It didn't take the RRU long to fix the hole—a quick melt seal did it. We can do permanent repairs at our leisure."

"Leisure," he scoffed. They had no time for leisure. From now until they defeated the Kindarians on their home world in the center of the Black Nebula, no one could expect the slightest respite.

"You worry too much, Cap'n. It'll get done," Barse promised.

He turned to Trahnee and Liottey. The first officer snored even louder now that the ship's cat had crawled into the man's lap, making a pillow of his leg.

"They will sleep for some time," Trahnee said.

"You talked to the cat, too?"

She smiled and shook her head.

"I had no need of that. The cat does nothing but eat, sleep and—"

"Let's get into the infirmary," Norlin cut in. "I want to see if we've still got a prisoner."

They found the Kindarian unfolding his eight limbs and stretching as if awakening from a long sleep. Its compound eyes stared expressionlessly at Norlin. He leveled the laserifle to let the spider-like being know escape was not possible.

His finger tensed on the weapon's firing stud. Too many memories flooded back when he saw this creature. World after human world had been laid waste by the alien's Death Fleet. A hard lump formed in Norlin's throat as he remembered Neela Cosarrian, her sea-green eyes and laughing manner, and the love they had shared. She had died in a Kindarian attack.

He thought of the ruined worlds and mutilated people, and the battles he and the *Preceptor*'s crew had fought against the aliens. To kill this one meant little, but it would give him a sense of finally retaliating, of striking back.

"Do not," Trahnee said softly. He felt the full intensity of her genhanced voice playing with his emotions, driving away the hurt and rage and restoring his sense of duty. This alien was worth more to the Empire Service alive than dead. Information was a rare commodity. He had the chance to find out needed details about the Kindarians—how they lived, how they died, why they attacked in their vicious, well-coordinated fashion.

"I won't. The idea is tempting, though," he admitted.

He prodded the alien and checked him quickly. For all the sudden loss of atmosphere, it seemed none the worse for the decompression. Kindarians might appear fragile, even spindly, but they were tough. From personal experience, he knew they were also incredibly strong. This one had been wounded and still fought like ten men.

"Tell us how you feel," urged Trahnee, kneeling beside the Kindarian.

The spider creature turned his dark compound eyes on her and said nothing.

"The loss of pressure might have ruptured his voice box," said Norlin.

"He can speak," Trahnee said positively. "I can feel the words trying to rush forth, to let us know what we seek." She gently drew the alien's antennae from their protective sheath in the carapace and stroked them. The way they quivered convinced Norlin the alien could hear.

If Trahnee was right, the Kindarian was hardly the worse physically for his escape attempt. Defeating his kind would be very hard, indeed.

"No," the Kindarian croaked. "I will not tell you more. You cannot force me. Kill me! I want to die a warrior's death!"

"Why do you pillage the planets like you do?" asked Norlin.

He had always wondered why the aliens slashed and burned and looted, making no attempt at colonization. The worlds they destroyed were prime, and planets capable of sustaining higher life forms were rare in the galaxy. More light years than he cared to think about separated the colonial worlds along the frontier.

"We do not deal with your kind," the Kindarian said.

"Why not?" Trahnee asked in her softly seductive tone. Norlin felt the subsonics quiver and rattle inside his eardrums. Genetically enhanced, she had other talents he could only guess at. This one was obvious. Trahnee spoke, and others obeyed.

Norlin barely listened to the Kindarian's response. His mind drifted back to first meeting Trahnee and her brother Bo Delamier. Insurrectionists, the pair of them. They had been banished from Emperor Arian's court on Earth because they sought his overthrow once too often.

Given all the stories he had heard about the emperor, Norlin wondered what the man was really like.

The genhanced officers he had met along the frontier had been demented. Usually brilliant but always showing a fatal flaw, they made life turn to death more often than not. Captain Pensky, for example, had commanded the *Preceptor* for less than a week. He had turned on his own ships and wrought havoc that permitted the Kindarian Death Fleet to destroy still another world.

In the middle of battle, though, Pensky had shown nothing less than genius in his tactics. Norlin occasionally reran the record of those brief encounters to study how Pensky had turned a single cruiser into the nemesis for a dozen ships, each with twice the *Preceptor*'s firepower.

"You cannot be trusted," the alien said. His mandibles clacked ominously. Norlin snapped back to the moment and touched the aiming stud on the laserifle. A tiny red bead shone brightly against the Kindarian's thorax, showing the precise spot where the beam would slice through him.

"What do you mean?" asked Trahnee. "When have you tried to deal with humanity? Have you spoken with Emperor Arian or someone in his court? Have you been to the foot of the Crystal Throne and spoken with our leaders?"

"Crystal Throne? I do not understand. We do not have to talk to your face to know your treachery," the alien said. "Witnessing your destruction of other creatures unlike yourselves is enough evidence. The probability is high that you would have dealt with us in the same fashion."

"You decided to strike at us before we could attack you?" asked Norlin.

He granted that humanity's record of contact with other intelligent species had been dismal. Three other than humanity had been discovered; two were almost annihilated because of unfortunate misunderstandings. Their numbers now were few, and they seldom strayed from their homeworlds.

Still, this reaction struck him as overly paranoid on the Kindarians' part. The third race, the Prothasians, were small, furry beasts the emperor held in high esteem—or so read the reports Norlin had seen.

From other things he had heard about Arian, he wondered about the nature of that esteem. Neither the other races nor any human settled world along the frontier enjoyed such attention.

"You are brutal. We saw high probability that you would kill us if we tried to negotiate." The Kindarian crouched down and wrapped his spidery legs around his main body protectively.

Norlin didn't know how to respond. These aliens had watched Earthmen conduct their affairs among the stars and had drawn a conclusion he might have himself. Earth sent vessels on their missions and direct scouting ventures into likely systems. The frontier worlds were too poor to expend such effort on a systematic basis—most frontier societies struggled under the burden of simply colonizing vast and empty worlds, often forced to extensively terraform more dangerous planets. Even the hospitable worlds carried dangers that required correction.

Empire Service exploratory ships fired first and talked later—the worlds along the star frontier had protested this often. It did no good.

Still, Norlin had to admit that not many colonists would argue too loudly against extermination of an alien race. They had come from the inner worlds and jealously protected their own planets from both new human and potential alien immigration. Such isolationism left any real opposition to the Kindarians up to the empire.

"If I assume you're right in your assessment of us, and I'm not..." Norlin shot a quick look at Trahnee. He couldn't read the expression on the genhanced woman's face, but he caught a flicker of amusement behind those grey eyes. She and the emperor shared much in their notions of entertainment, he concluded. "If we assume you're right, why are you so systematically looting our worlds? Why not attack and colonize?"

"That is not our way. We must eradicate. That is Kindarian destiny. It is beneath us to grub about like you do."

The prisoner made a choking noise. Norlin thought the creature had something caught in his throat until he saw the mandible clacking and the leg twitching that went along with the sound.

"He exhibits extreme hostility," Trahnee said needlessly. "He is contemptuous of us."

"He might be scornful," said Norlin, "but we captured him. We destroyed his ship along with many more in his flotilla."

"The Death Fleet will continue to cut through your civilization until you are brought to your knees."

"You've declared war on us?" Norlin was puzzled by the Kindarian's reaction.

"War? We do not understand war. We defend ourselves. We live as the Supreme intends those of Kindar to live. Any other lifestyle is beneath our contempt." The alien's haughtiness convinced Norlin they weren't likely to get new information.

"Any more?" he asked Trahnee.

"What do you want from him? He will be…amenable," she said. He felt the vibrancy in her voice. She wanted to toy with the prisoner, to force him to speak against his will. In her way, Trahnee delighted in baiting the Kindarian. If she played with the alien's mind, Norlin wondered whether Emperor Arian would go further and indulge his reputed sadistic tendencies with physical torture, for the amusement of his court.

He would do more than just ask questions, Norlin suspected.

Norlin motioned for Trahnee to leave. The Kindarian glared at them, his eyes flashing with a million facets of reflected hatred. Norlin touched his com-link.

"Barse, make sure our elusive friend doesn't try to wander again. Put a couple robots on patrol in the corridor and in compartments around him. I don't give a damn if he tries to chew his way into space."

"It might be for the best, Cap'n. How long we going to coddle him?" came the engineer's immediate response.

"We need him," Norlin said. "The emperor has to see something substantive to support our reports of an alien death fleet."

"Let him see the worlds they've ruined," grumbled Barse.

Norlin clicked off his com-link. He paced the corridor slowly, each step echoing like a peal of a funeral bell.

"Emperor Arian might not have received any of the messages sent," Trahnee said. "He is very…unreceptive on some topics. This would be one, I fear."

"Admiral Bendo sent no fewer than a dozen message packets to Earth, all filled with documentation of the Kindarian invasion," said Norlin. "My reports on the first depredations have been circulated widely along the frontier."

"I am sure the report has reached the emperor's court," Trahnee said. "That does not mean anyone took it seriously." She laid her hand on his shoulder. He stopped. Her eyes bored into his pale-violet ones. "Do you think Emperor Arian will look at your captive and agree to invasion of the Black Nebula?"

"He has to," Norlin said. "The frontier has no other chance for survival. *Earth* has no other chance." Hope eluded him that any of the emperor's gengineered advisors would agree.

# Chapter Three

Enemy ships closing fast! Array of genius missiles on their way! We're heading into a passive mine field!" Pier Norlin snapped out the problems as he tapped them into his command computer. His heads-up display helmet flashed red warnings all around him.

A small movement of his chin turned off the mock display. He turned and stared at his communications officer as she fought to detect all the incoming missiles.

Chikako Miza's scalplock glowed with red and green and amber. Some nanowires ran directly into her head, finding neural connector points in her brain to give instant linkage with her equipment. Other wiring went to transmitters cunningly hung as jewelry from ears and throat. Chikako was a living com-link. But he was often overloaded simply with visual displays. Didn't so much direct input confuse her?

As she put every circuit at her disposal to work on the tactical problem, she spoke quietly and steadily. Her fingers worked across her com board as she did the work of a half-dozen officers. Direct connect, auditory and tactile—her command and control tripled what Norlin achieved.

From her board poured the flood of data Mitri Sarov needed to counter the threat to the *Preceptor*. The tactical officer cast a huge shadow across his controls as he hunched forward, thick fingers punching and tuning, probing and gently coercing impossible defensives from the ship's active combat systems.

"Got trouble, Cap'n," came Tia Barse's voice in Norlin's headphones. "Tickler unit is acting up. We can't excite the fusion torch enough to up the power to fire the radiation cannon. If we try, we'll blow everything across the board."

"Compensate," Norlin ordered Sarov. "We can't use the radiation cannon. Lay down a defensive barrage. If we run, they'll turn us into expanding gas in seconds."

"Done."

Norlin wondered what would excite Sarov. The man never showed emotion at his post. Only during the card games with Barse did he betray any agitation. Barse always beat him—he owed her months of pay. Norlin wanted to tell him to use the same emotional control during combat when he played. That way, Barse couldn't read him as easily as she did.

Norlin shrugged it off. Losing at cards might be Sarov's way of relieving tension. He dared not make a mistake in situations like this one. Even though computers did most of the work—they had the femtosecond response times humans lacked—an organic brain had to guide and provide the inspiration rather than imitating his computers with their souless prognostications.

Sarov was the best Norlin had seen during his limited time in the Empire Service. He was glad he had him for tactical officer.

He smiled crookedly. He was glad he had them *all*, even Gowan Liottey, although that stretched his acceptance to the breaking point. The *Preceptor* had been a prize when he gained command of it by outliving the other line officers. Although he had lacked experience, he had the flare for command that kept such diverse personalities welded together as a team—and alive.

So far.

"We can power up the lasartillery now.," Barse reported. "Still can't use the radiation cannon. We've got problems with the switching circuit."

Norlin worked his controls, adding new problems to the exercise. Having Sarov use the lasartillery seemed appropriate;

he wanted to see if the tac officer was depending too much on the captured Kindarian radiation cannon.

New parameters for the battle problem flashed across Norlin's vidscreen. He added and subtracted to give the entire crew a complete test of their abilities. To his surprise, even Gowan Liottey responded well.

The first officer's usual role was life support systems maintenance, a job normally filled by robots during combat. Liottey had so few other talents, Norlin had thought it safer to keep him occupied with routine tasks.

No longer. Liottey worked to full potential now with robots on the life support system and evaluating expertly what damage required immediate attention and what repairs could be postponed. The RRUs had never been handled better, even by Tia Barse.

Norlin smiled when he saw the ninety-five-percent confidence levels returning for Liottey, Barse and Chikako Miza. Mitri Sarov tallied a full ninety-seven percent, better than all but a handful of officers in the Empire Service.

When the *Preceptor* went into the Black Nebula to hunt Kindarians and locate their homeworld, the ship would be more than a match for anything the aliens threw in their orbit.

Norlin ran a few new problems by them to compound the difficulty of the combat test. They responded well. One by one, the red lights turned amber and finally winked a green to indicate successful termination.

"Cap'n, you still running a test on me or is the tickler really showing instability in its output?" Tia Barse's voice told him that the question—and problem—was real.

"Test is terminating now," he said, removing the last of the ersatz alien warships from the computer. Space around them for dozens of light minutes was free of any other vessel. He checked his master readout then moved his chin switch to get more comprehensive details. Barse had picked up a small output problem at its inception.

"Still got it, Cap'n. What do you want me to do?"

"All hands, all hands," he said. "Full repair authorized. If you've got any glitches, erase them. Barse, divert however many RRUs you need for repair."

"Sir, do you want the robots standing guard over the Kindarian diverted to the engine compartment?" came Liottey's question. The confidence in his voice startled Norlin. He was used to a whining, self-deprecating tone from the first officer.

"What are you suggesting, Mr. Liottey?"

"Let Barse have the RRUs. I'll watch the prisoner. He seems afraid of me after my outburst."

Norlin touched the computer toggle to get Liottey's medical readout. A quick scan revealed the man's vitals. Gowan Liottey had recovered past his recorded norms.

"Do so," Norlin said, glad to be able to shift some command responsibility to his first officer. Even an automated ship like the *Preceptor* needed humans to keep it functioning. Sharing the authority for routine procedures rather than tending to it all himself allowed him to prepare for the battles to come.

He wasn't sure entering the Black Nebula and fighting the Kindarian Death Fleet was the hardest part of the one-sided war, either. First, he had to take the cruiser to Earth and convince Emperor Arian of the threat. That might prove more difficult than anything he had yet undertaken.

"I'm almost at maximum efficiency," reported Sarov. "There's not much more I can do with this setup of computers and control equipment."

"Any chance for improvement with a different configuration?" asked Norlin. He'd heard the tiny quiver of plaintive request in Sarov's voice. The tac officer wanted to make changes to their system. Empire Service regulations were precise on this point— it was never to be done. To allow one ship to alter fire control systems meant chaos during coordinated, close-fleet maneuvers.

"Do what you want, Mitri," Norlin said. Central command relaying orders from distant Earth would prove suicidal in real combat with the Kindarian fleet; the time delay, the high-command arguments over tactics, the political infighting for access to the emperor had to be circumvented. He saw no reason it should not start with his ship. Now.

"Barse, what's the condition of the radiation cannon?"

He knew this weapon, more than anything else aboard the *Preceptor*, elevated them above Empire Service standards and strategy. They had taken the Kindarian radiation cannon from a damaged scout ship after an engagement but had been unable to use it except as a one-shot weapon because of the drain it put on their power system. A chance battle in the Porlock system had given them the switch the Kindarians used to prevent the massive power depletion. Theirs now matched the armament of the smaller ships in the Kindarian Death Fleet.

Norlin tried not to think of the massive planet wreckers the aliens had. Those outgunned the heaviest ships in the Empire Service fleet.

The engineer's voice came crisply in his headphones.

"In perfect condition, Cap'n. You want a test firing?"

"Not until your engines are at full capacity," he said.

"We're almost there. The RRUs Liottey freed up are about finished. We're in damned good shape."

"Pleased to hear it," Norlin said dryly. He lounged back in the command chair and relaxed for the first time in longer than he could remember. Command weighed heavily on him. As far as he knew, the *Preceptor* was the only cruiser to engage in single combat with the alien death fleet and survive. Entire *planets* had died. Only when Admiral Bendo drew the line at Sutton and fought with both ground and space forces did the Death Fleet meet its match.

He watched the command computer race through systems checks. Everything was in perfect condition. How long would this last once they engaged the Death Fleet again? Not long, he knew, but they would cut a swath all the way to the Kindarians' homeworld in the Black Nebula.

"Let's set course for Alpha Centauri," he said.

He looked over his shoulder. Trahnee nodded agreement with his decision. Alpha Centauri was the oldest of Earth's colonies and provided a gateway to the home solar system—Emperor Arian ordered destroyed any vessel entering Earth space without permission.

Norlin had another reason for not going directly to Earth. He wanted to see if Trahnee and her brother had been forgotten. He had never pressed the woman to learn why she had been exiled to the frontier rather than executed outright for inciting a revolt to overthrow Arian. He knew he might find out the hard way, blundering through the political maze that Earth had become, but for now ignorance was preferable. Broaching the subject made him very nervous. He loved Trahnee and did not like the idea that she was a traitor to the empire.

"Shift engines ready?"

He received confirmation from Barse. A quick survey of the others showed the *Preceptor* was ready. He locked in the destination, and the powerful shift engines jerked them out of normal space and into the nothingness between dimensions that allowed faster-than-light travel.

"We're on our way," he said, more to himself than to Trahnee and his crew.

"We will convince Arian," Trahnee assured him. "I need to speak to him personally, but he will be convinced of your need."

"It's not *my* need," Norlin said irritably. "The Kindarians are pillaging *all* worlds. I still don't understand why they destroy and rush on the way they do—it's enough that they do it. This isn't something for just the frontier worlds to worry over. It's for the emperor. After all, he's supposed to be in charge."

He didn't like Trahnee's answering sardonic laugh.

✳ ✳ ✳

"We're cleared for entry," Chikako Miza announced. "I'm picking up a loud signal, though. I don't like it."

"What's the nature of the signal?" asked Norlin, more intent on recognition codes and finding the proper traffic clearance plans for the space station circling Alpha Centauri V. The worlds of this star system were uniformly barren. Three-hundred-eighty years of planetary reconstruction had only started turning the fifth rocky, lifeless globe into a livable site.

Circling the world was the largest station Norlin had ever seen, however. Supporting such a base required more effort than colonizing a dozen worlds along the frontier.

"I've tuned a receiver for the Kindarian frequencies. That's one of their squeals. There's a microburst transmission being sent from inside this system, Captain."

Norlin cancelled the swiftly changing approach information the computer was furnishing and concentrated on Chikako's com board. The readouts confirmed all she had said. They were picking up tiny leakages from Kindarian broadcasts.

"They're here already," he said, tiredness descending over him like a thick, suffocating blanket. He had hoped the heart of the empire would be immune from the aliens' overwhelming devastation.

"The exterior sensors are theirs," said Sarov. "I've identified no fewer than five they have replaced. Their method of attack is unchanged."

"Why not?" Norlin slumped even more in the command chair. "They've got a blueprint that works. Replace the sensors, lull the stupid humans into believing we're invincible, then sneak in. By the time forces can be rallied, the bulk of the Death Fleet is turning radiation cannon on the worlds and whatever defenders have reached space."

"I can alert the space station," said Trahnee. "I can *make* them believe there is danger."

"Try," he said, but he didn't think she would be successful.

After the controller refused to patch her through to his superior, Norlin knew what they had to do.

"We're breaking off. We're going alien hunting. Chikako, drop a message packet onto the com officer aboard the space station. Mitri, microburst a complete analysis of the Kindarian attack model to their battle ops officer. Barse, get us ready for combat. Full power on the engines. We'll need it."

"What do we do with the prisoner?" came from Liottey.

"Chain him up. I need you on the bridge, Gowan."

"Aye, sir. Right away. I've found a three-oh-four carbon steel his digestive juices can't corrode."

"Lock him up and get here immediately."

Trahnee put her hand on his shoulder.

"Let me try once more. I might be able to sway the controller."

"No," he said. "There's a filter on the circuit. Your particular talent doesn't affect him." He saw the sorrow on her face. He shucked the command helmet and kissed her quickly. "Stay on the bridge. We might have to contact other Empire Service ships. We can use all the help we can get tracking down the Kindarian scout ships infiltrating the system."

"So close to Earth," she said, heaving a deep sigh. "I am sorry now that Bo and I were not more successful in our attempts to overthrow Emperor Arian. Bo enjoyed war games. We would have had patrols out constantly."

Norlin didn't know how to answer her.

He put the command helmet back on and began laying in a course that would take them sweeping across the Alpha Centauri system then through the interface space between Alpha and the M-class red dwarf Proxima almost ten thousand AUs distant. Norlin checked the positions of the sensor posts and cursed. The standard dispersion pattern had been used, making their location an easy target for the Kindarian scouts.

"We know where to look," Chikako pointed out, almost as if she had read his mind. "What works for them works for us, too."

"Optimal course," Norlin said, finishing the trajectory through the system. "Keep a sharp eye out for any sign of their scout ships."

To his surprise, Gowan Liottey made the first reading on an enemy ship.

"Less than five light-minutes away, Captain," the first officer barked out. "There's a sensor planted on the cometary object. The Kindarian is hiding behind it, keeping the bulk of the ice between us and him."

"How did you get it?" asked Norlin. Neither Chikako nor Sarov had picked up any radiation leaks from the other ship.

"Heat profile," came the immediate answer. "The Kindarian ship melts part of the comet. The shimmer of water vapor indicates a higher temperature than should exist. The scout has to be hiding behind the snowball."

"It might be an anomaly," said Chikako Miza.

"Then let's check it out for its scientific value," Norlin said.

Less than a minute later the mass spectrometer picked up telltale exhaust products from a Kindarian engine.

"Got him," said Sarov. "Caught sight of his nose as he edged around the comet head to sneak a look at us."

"Prepare for battle," Norlin said softly.

His heart raced, but he kept himself under control. To lose now meant the entire system would fall. From here it was an easy 4.2 light-year jaunt to Earth. He flipped a toggle and got a com-link with the Alpha Centauri space station. Chikako nodded, indicating he had an untappable laser linkage. He spoke quickly as he relayed the situation on the outskirts of the system.

"…can't dignify that with a response, *Preceptor*," came the choppy reply. "Enemy? Alien invasion? We get space dust like that all the time from the colonies. There's no evidence other than you going crazy."

Norlin switched to vidscreen circuit and relayed the image of the alien scout ship edging around the comet. As he did so he saw not one but two Death Fleet ships.

"We've got a fight on our hands. Get us support immediately." He toggled off before the space station controller could reply.

"There's three of them!" Chikako Miza cried out.

Pier Norlin said nothing. He worked feverishly on his command computer to ready the *Preceptor* for battle. He entered the last of his combat orders none too soon. Missiles snaked across space toward them, and laser beams sought their hull.

The war for human survival had begun.

# Chapter Four

I 've got them," Mitri Sarov reported in his bass tones. "All missiles interdicted. A response array is on its way back to them."

"Lasartillery fire at will," ordered Norlin. He knew Sarov had already programmed the automatic weapons to fire but felt he had to do something. Too much of the battle was out of his hands. Watching the ebb and flow and trying to outguess his opponents was the true nature of his job.

He did strategy, Sarov worked his magic on the tactical front. Norlin hoped he could uphold his end of the battle planning without meddling. Studying the patterns required no immediate action on his part, but not actively fighting was *hard*.

"One scout damaged," came Liottey's report. "A missile came up from behind and exploded in its engine."

"The other two ships are chattering," said Chikako Miza. "They didn't think they would be detected. My impression is they're going to run rather than fight."

"Lay down a volley of missiles to stop them. I want them all destroyed. No one leaves the system!"

The *Preceptor* shivered as another round of genius missiles hurtled toward the Kindarian scout ships. The missiles corrected in midflight, decided on different tactics and implemented them. Each deadly missile had to be coped with separately by the alien defenses. Simple kinetic barrages were not sufficient to stop them as their vectors constantly changed.

"Scout destroyed," cried Liottey. "The one that Sarov hit is gone. I'm reading the spectroscopics on the debris around the comet."

"No good," corrected Sarov. "That's an old trick. They released gas and solid debris to make you think one was gone. All three remain in fighting condition. Count on it."

Norlin fired the radiation cannon directly into the icy comet. The ammonia ice and carbon dioxide boiled away in a twinkling cloud of rapidly expanding vapor. The three Kindarian scouts were silhouetted by the hot, sputtering gases.

"Locked on all three." Sarov said as he worked.

The *Preceptor*'s computer automatically fired the radiation cannon as soon as it had powered up again. Two blasts from the conventional lasartillery and a corkscrewing nuclear-tipped missile disposed of the nearest alien scout. Another spun away out of control, a gaping hole blown in its side. Sarov sent a fresh volley of implacable missiles after it. The sudden flare on the vidscreen four minutes later showed the tac officer's expertise in choosing just the right combination for maximum destruction.

"One left," said Norlin. He frowned as he studied the computer readout on the ship. The alien's course showed it closing on them for attack. This didn't surprise him. That the alien came directly for the *Preceptor* did. The Empire Service ship had just destroyed its two companions. Why did its commander think he could do one-on-one battle and win?

"Veer off," Norlin said, coming to a quick decision. "Keep up a defensive screen of missiles. This one's got something hot aboard. He wants us to engage."

"We can take him!" protested Sarov.

"Unusual heat signature," said Liottey, still manning the small bank of scientific equipment mounted outside the ship. "He's hotter."

"The son of a bitch is going to suicide!"

Norlin wasn't sure who spoke. It might have been Sarov or it might even have been a frightened Miza. His fingers played an arpeggio across the computer as he set up new tactics. The ship shuddered as it swung about on its axis. The prow was pointed directly at the enemy vessel when it exploded.

"Hot gas, some debris, heavy radiation," reported Liottey. "I've got a spectrum reading on it. Heavy on the x-ray side. Shielding around the bridge handled it. Barse is all right in the engine compartment—the length of the *Preceptor* shielded her."

"What of the prisoner?" asked Trahnee.

Norlin checked. The Kindarian prisoner remained huddled in his cell, welded steel cuffs holding four of his legs firmly to the deck plates. Other than the imprisonment, the spider-like creature seemed unharmed.

"He can take far higher radiation levels than we can," he decided. "He's like an Earth spider. There isn't much inside them that's complicated enough to be destroyed by ionizing radiation."

He started to say more then clamped his mouth shut. What of the Kindarian's brain? That had to be as complex and radiation-susceptible as a human brain. He had to push aside such speculation. There was too much else to do right now.

"I've recorded the entire encounter," said Liottey. "Do you think it'll convince the controller back at the station that we know what we're talking about?"

Norlin kept his ship's sensors strained to their limit in a vain effort to find other alien ships sneaking into the system. He confirmed only the debris left from their short but fierce battle.

He didn't hold much hope that Liottey's vid of the battle would convince any of the Empire Service officers, either. They were too cocksure that the defensive warning network around Alpha Centauri—and Earth—was impenetrable, and that their only possible invasion threat came from the colonies along the frontier.

"Let's not bother with the controller," he decided. "We're going straight for Earth and the emperor."

"But, Pier," protested Trahnee. "They will destroy us the instant we shift in!"

He shook his head. The Empire Service warships had never taken defensive positions in this system. He didn't think those allegedly protecting Earth would be any more efficient.

He commanded the tightest, nastiest fighting ship in human-controlled space. The emperor's best couldn't stand against the *Preceptor*.

"We're going to Earth," he said firmly. "Now."

He set course and prepared to shift.

## \* \* \*

"They're threatening to blow us out of space if we attempt to go to Earth without clearance," said Chikako Miza. She tipped her head to one side and listened to other conversations on other circuits. "They want to know what happened out toward Proxima."

"Send them another message packet," ordered Norlin. "Any chance they can stop us from shifting?"

"None," came Sarov's gruff voice. "They have nothing in space that can touch us. I thought the Empire Service ships at the frontier were lax. These are..." Words failed the burly tac officer. He was used to heaping scorn on his fellows. For these ships, he lacked properly denigrating utterances.

"Barse, are we ready to shift?" Norlin studied the long columns of numbers detailing the power and drive subsystems' status. He saw nothing awry but wanted verification. He got it.

"Trahnee?" he asked.

"We should wait for clearance," she said. "I can deal with them. Let's meet face-to-face. They cannot deny me then."

"We have information vital to the survival of the empire. Spending a month or longer getting petty bureaucrats to agree to let us continue to Earth does nothing but waste time and doom more colony worlds."

"Colonies, Captain?" asked Gowan Liottey. "We've just seen the vanguard of the Kindarian invasion thrust into the heart of the empire. They have to know Alpha Centauri is only a stepping stone to Earth. If they attack here, they'll arrive at Earth within days."

"Hours," grumbled Sarov. "They don't need to do more than demolish the Alphacent space station. There aren't any planets to beam into submission."

"Prepare to shift for Earth. To hell with the controller's protests." Norlin turned to Trahnee and asked, "What is he likely to do when we shift out?"

She shrugged. "How can I say? No one disobeys the emperor's controller this close to the Crystal Throne. Surprise might be on your side."

"What happens when we reach the solar system?"

She shook her head. Such questions had never been seriously asked before.

Norlin smiled crookedly. If the questions had never been asked, perhaps no one defending Earth had answers. With a spot of luck, he might win through Earth controllers and to Emperor Arian himself. The Death Fleet had to be stopped now that it threatened the core of the human settled stars.

"Message packet away?"

"Aye, Captain," said Chikako.

"Course locked in. Let's shift for Earth."

The rush of senses-disorienting energy flooded past; Norlin blinked and kept working to minimize its effect. It took only minutes for him to verify their course. The journey to Earth would be short, unlike the myriad light-years-long stretches between colony worlds along the frontier.

Ten minutes later, alarms flashed, and the *Preceptor* prepared to drop back into regular space. Slightly more than four light-years had passed at top speed.

"We're ready, Cap'n," reported Barse. "The cat's in his box, and the engines are purring as contented as can be."

Norlin nodded, although the engineer couldn't see him. The readouts glowing centimeters in front of his face confirmed everything Barse said. The *Preceptor* had been a hot ship when he took it over. In the ensuing months, he had squeezed the best from both crew and equipment. Nothing even in the Nova Class could touch his vessel.

"Com everywhere. Space is buzzing," said Chikako. "No attempt at scrambling or laser linkage."

Norlin switched to the external sensors. The ship's detectors picked up a fleet moving in crazy orbits throughout the solar system.

"Analysis," he barked.

For several seconds, no one spoke. He swung around and stared across the bridge at Chikako and Sarov. Both simply sat and stared at their boards.

"Liottey?"

"I don't know what to make of it, Captain," the first officer said. "There's enough firepower around us to destroy a dozen Death Fleets. Your message packet must have stirred them up to send such a fleet into space."

"Heavy armament around us, aye," confirmed Sarov, "but the ships aren't in any battle formation."

"Can it be a new tactic some genhanced line officer is trying?" asked Norlin.

"I could pick off a dozen of them before anyone knew what was going on," said Sarov. "I can't believe this is a planned exercise."

Norlin ran the other ships' trajectories through his own battle computer and came to the same conclusion. For all the energy being expended rushing from one side of the solar system to the other, for all the lasartillery and missiles being fired, it was all sound and fury and signified nothing.

He laid in a low-energy orbit sunward toward Earth. By creating as little stir as possible among the other Empire Service ships, he hoped to avoid detection. Whatever caused such frantic activity on their part meant nothing to him but a chance to deliver his message unhindered.

"Can they be preparing to defend the system against the Death Fleet?" asked Liottey. "I don't know what to make of this, Captain. Please help me to understand."

Norlin swung around and blanked his heads-up display for a moment to stare at his first officer. Liottey had never asked for instruction before. He had always been too busy protesting, whining, venting his anger at what he couldn't change.

The CoolinGas had done more than scramble Liottey's brains. It had improved his attitude.

"They might be, but I don't think so," said Norlin. "They're spread too thin to meet any major incursion. Check your computer."

He flashed a complete stochastic analysis of the patterns onto Liottey's small vidscreen, showing the way most ships were out of position to efficiently counter any significant, coordinated attack.

"Should we contact fleet com and see what's happening?" asked Chikako. "This might be an emergency."

Norlin looked at Trahnee. The genhanced woman stood to one side of the control room, her face pale. She watched the darting figures on Liottey's vidscreen. From her horrified expression, she knew what was happening.

"Trahnee," Norlin asked softly. "What is it? What are they doing?"

"Training," she said in a choked voice. "Emperor Arian is conducting a training maneuver."

"What kind of maneuver is *that*?" protested Sarov. "Damn, one just opened up on another. There must be a mutiny in the fleet. How can we tell who are the rebels and which are still loyal to the Service? And does it matter to us?"

"They're all loyal," Trahnee said, her voice threatening to break with strain. "You don't understand. The emperor calls it training. It isn't. He's sent the entire fleet out to…practice."

"On each other?" Norlin couldn't understand the purpose. Training might be brutal, but it was never purposefully destructive of your own forces.

His stomach felt as if it accelerated through shift space as he came to the realization that he was wrong. Arian *did* destroy his own fleet by pitting one segment against another. He did it for the sick pleasure such death and carnage brought him.

"Yes, Pier," Trahnee said. "He enjoys it more than anything else. He is sitting on the Crystal Throne now and watching a huge vidscreen at the far end of his audience chamber."

"How long does it go on?" demanded Sarov. "Two heavy cruisers have just been turned into plasma." The waste of such equipment—and crews—appalled him.

"The emperor declares different rules for each training session. The worst continue until there are only a prescribed number of ships remaining."

"The battleships have a definite advantage in that," muttered Norlin.

Instinctively, he sought out the heaviest ships the Empire Service had in space. Too many of them were near the *Preceptor*. If they came after him, retreat was his only option. He began setting up the parameters for a shift away from the Earth system.

"That would leave only one class of warships," agreed Trahnee. "That is why he changes the rules. Sometimes the scouts are favored. Speed, maneuverability, energy efficiency are the goals. Still other times it is a giant race. Ships must complete a circuit around the system and return before any of the others."

"That sounds more like a training exercise," said Norlin.

Trahnee shook her head. Her dark hair spilled forward into her eyes. She brushed it aside with a nervous gesture unlike her.

"All ships are allowed to complete the course in any fashion they want. The battleships are still favored; the smaller ships take heavy losses."

"The emperor's a madman," grumbled Barse over the comlink to the engine room. "Why are we trying to save his ass? Let's get back to the frontier and rally support against the Kindarians. The colony worlds can put as good a fleet into space as anything we're likely to find here."

Norlin almost agreed. The reason intruded heavily over his emotions.

"The invasion of the Black Nebula isn't something that can be successful with a handful of ships each vying for individual victory. You know how it is among the frontier worlds."

"We don't need the Empire Service fleet. There might not be anything left after they finish this." Barse cut the circuit and left Norlin to think.

He came to the conclusion he had earlier—the emperor's cooperation was needed. The colony worlds could not survive independent of the empire, and the empire would fall with a knife through its heart unless the Kindarians' homeworld was destroyed first. To amass the fleet needed for the task, the Empire Service had to back the invasion.

"We're going to Earth," he said. "Try to avoid the heavier ships. Return fire, if necessary. Use defensive missiles and lasartillery until otherwise ordered."

"Pier, we won't make it. Each vessel receives points for destroying another in such games." Trahnee looked stricken. Norlin wondered if she was changing her attitudes. He loved her, in spite of a hard center of selfishness running through her. Was she actually worried about the *Preceptor* and its crew? Or did she fear her own death if he insisted on seeing the emperor?

"Those are their orders," he said. "We don't get points for destroying our allies."

The vidscreen blazed with destruction now. They had shifted into the solar system at the beginning of the vicious self-extermination games. Norlin hoped the emperor went blind watching such good men and women slaughtered at his whim.

He worked to get the *Preceptor* inward of Saturn's orbit and to the space station circling Earth. Carefully avoiding the larger ships, he corkscrewed over and under the asteroids and thought he had made the perilous journey unscathed when alarms flashed up and down his board.

"Midget battleship detected," barked out Chikako Miza. "Closing fast."

"Full defensives out. They pushed our ECM missile array aside. We're using lasartillery to the fullest. We're beginning to overload. They're throwing everything at us. We're their only target." Sarov's dour voice carried a load of gloom with it. Norlin saw why as he studied the readouts dashing in front of his face. The heads-up display gave him only the highlights of his officers' reports.

He went cold inside when the ship's sensors picked up the visual on the midget battleship.

"That's Emperor Arian's personal ship," he muttered. "We're facing the best ship in the whole damned Empire Service fleet!"

The *Preceptor* rocked as a missile slipped past Sarov's defensive screen and blew apart a forward cabin. Airtights screamed closed, and the robot repair units whirred to work.

For a few seconds Pier Norlin sat and stared at the vidscreen. Then he, too, went to work. Emperor's flagship or not, he wasn't going to allow the *Preceptor* to be destroyed without a fight.

# Chapter Five

I can't figure out what he's doing to get to us like that!" Mitri Sarov was as agitated as Norlin had ever seen him. The tactical officer's thick fingers flew so fast over his computer keyboard they blurred.

Norlin tilted his head to one side and watched the quick-step of numbers racing through the officer's display. He nodded slowly, understanding what Sarov was asking of the *Preceptor*'s battle computer. The heads-up display vanished as he moved his head. He tipped his head back and regained the tactical display.

"We can avoid most of what's being thrown at us," he told Sarov, "if we use the lasartillery instead of missiles to intercept. They must have a new attack algorithm built into their missiles. We're missing them by centimeters with our defensives."

The *Preceptor* shuddered as another genius missile sneaked past their defenses. Norlin momentarily switched from tactical display to repair. He smiled broadly when he saw that Gowan Liottey was tending to the necessary patching with an efficiency worthy of a top officer in the Empire Service. Norlin was only sorry it had taken brain damage and extreme pain from the CoolinGas accident to cause this change in his first officer.

They would need every bit of ability available to avoid destruction by the emperor's flagship.

"That's working. We needed the extra speed. They've got a different configuration of steering jets on their missiles," decided Sarov. "I'm programming that into our computer now. We can probably avoid another barrage."

Norlin stabbed down hard on the lasartillery firing stud. The three forward batteries spewed unimaginable torrents of coherent light in an attempt to destroy the attacking midget battleship. The other vessel rolled along its axis and deflected the direct hit. Some light was reflected off by mirrors circling the ship; the rest was dissipated by the rapid rotation. Their lasers had little chance to superheat any portion of the thickly hulled warship.

"They know their job. They're good, too damned good," complained Chikako Miza. "I'm not even picking up chatter off their internal system com leakage."

Norlin listened as his officers discussed the battle and analyzed it with only a portion of his intellect. The greater portion of his attention was focused on the other ship. Chikako was right. That crew was different. They were the best he had ever fought.

The Kindarians relied on surprise and heavy specialization of their war craft; their heaviest battleships were nothing more than armor and massive radiation cannon. They could not maneuver well. Their scouts were quick and deadly—but defeatable. The emperor's midget battleship had the heavy armor and lasartillery of a planet-wrecker coupled with the maneuverability of a much smaller vessel.

"Where is the weakness?" Norlin wondered aloud. There had to be a soft spot.

But the crew reacted well to every new ploy tried by the *Preceptor*. The battleship was in perfect condition. He saw no weakness to hammer at. Even worse, he knew the officers were genhanced. They played with their brilliance the way others enjoyed games of chance.

"Let's get the hell out of here, Cap'n," came Barse's voice in his ears. "We can't keep up these levels of g-loading. You're straining our support members."

"We're not running," he said. "They'd be on us in an instant. We wouldn't have the time to prepare for a shift."

Even as he spoke, his fingers tapped in new instructions.

"Barse, get ready to cut power. We're going to simulate a powerless hulk. Chikako, plot their course down to a millimeter. Lock your sensors into the computer aiming the radiation cannon. Sarov, wait for the precise moment for a broadside to hit us before powering down the lasartillery."

"We can't!" the tactical officer protested. "They won't stand back and stare at us. They'll keep firing until we're atoms!"

Norlin knew he took a risk with this tactic. He counted on the genhanced officers' to pausing for an instant to gloat over their personal superiority before giving the order to devastate the apparently damaged *Preceptor*. The genhanced didn't lack the killer instinct, but they also had egos far out of proportion to the size of their accomplishments.

Pier Norlin hoped that was true this time. If he misjudged them, the *Preceptor* would be nothing but a cloud of expanding gas in a few seconds.

"We go black after the incoming volley. Sarov, take out all but one missile. Let it hit us."

"I protest. Any one of those missiles can blow us to hell and gone!"

"Do it." Norlin rechecked his figures. The *Preceptor* was a taut ship but could not withstand the punishment a battleship could give. Seeing the quickness of turns and how eagerly the inertial platforms on the other ship trained on target, he knew they could not outrun its destructive capacity, either.

"Captain, should I send a request to surrender?" asked Chikako. "That might further lull them into thinking we were dead in space."

"Do it. Mention an engine room failure. They can see there's nothing wrong with our launchers or lasartillery."

"They laughed, sir," came Chikako's immediate reply. "They *want* to destroy us."

That made Norlin's decision easier. He bobbed about as he studied the readouts in his heads-up display. Computer guidance for the radiation cannon was coupled with Chikako's long-range sensors. Sarov neatly picked off missile after missile with his cunning counter-programming.

"One's left," Sarov said glumly. "It'll hit somewhere around the infirmary."

"Damn it," muttered Norlin. He didn't want the alien killed. He needed him to bolster his claims when he stood before the Crystal Throne and Emperor Arian.

"We're committed," Sarov said. The burly man rocked back in his chair and stared at his vidscreen. The feathery scars under his left eye turned bright pink as blood pulsed into his face. A large vein throbbed at his temple.

Norlin watched the last act in the battle unfold in slow motion. Chikako tracked the missile all the way to strike amidships. Barse cut power the instant the explosion rattled their teeth and caused pressure loss throughout a quarter of the ship.

Sensors locked onto the midget battleship, still pointed prowfirst toward the *Preceptor* to present as tiny a target as possible. Norlin felt as if years passed. The battleship ceased fire the instant the ship's systems went down—why waste energy and valuable missiles on a lifeless hulk?

Norlin endured centuries as he watched the battleship fall out of full battle readiness and the captain exercise a momentary lapse. A thin crescent of ship's prow presented itself. He waited. More of the midget battleship hove into sensor view. He had set the parameters himself for firing the captured Kindarian radiation cannon. He had to have a clean kill. Nothing less would get them free of the emperor's flagship.

"There!" he heard Chikako cry. Sarov's grunt seemed an echo. The *Preceptor*'s engines powered a beam of unthinkable energy that ripped along the side of the battleship. Mirrors adequate for reflecting lasartillery strikes vaporized. The metal beneath simply vanished—and so did the crew and the ship around them.

"Ninety percent chance of a total kill," came Sarov's evaluation. "Request permission to use either lasartillery or another blast from the radiation cannon."

"Lasartillery," decided Norlin. "I want that ship beamed out of space. Reduce it to plasma."

His stomach heaved. He had no desire to kill any survivors, but he could not risk them signaling another, heavier ship for aid. He had watched Chikako's board and had picked up no distress call from the dying battleship.

The *Preceptor*'s lasartillery fired then fired again.

"It's metallic vapor," came Sarov's relieved voice. "We did it. We beat the emperor's best!"

Norlin went over the computerized damage reports. Barse had RRUs working in every section of the ship. Their hull had been penetrated in more than forty spots. Worst of all, they had lost a third of their cargo hold to the last missile. The cruiser dared not engage even the smallest of Kindarian scout ships without risking instant destruction until the hold and hull had been repaired.

That required complete dry dock facilities.

"Can we fight another ship?" asked Trahnee.

"We're in unstable condition," Norlin told her truthfully. "We can, but we'd probably lose if we came up against anything larger than a picket ship." He projected a phase space diagram onto the vidscreen showing their velocity versus time. They might achieve Earth orbit if they avoided all other encounters.

He held back his despair when two heavy cruisers, one Nebula Class and the other a twin to his own Nova Class *Preceptor*, set intercept courses. Both would attack long before the cruiser reached the dubious safety of Earth's orbit.

"Captain, I've detected a radio source close to Earth. I don't know what to make of it. I've never seen anything quite like it before." Chikako switched over the image to his vidscreen.

Norlin stared at the odd structure.

"It looks like a bull's-eye," said Liottey. "Do you think it's a finish line for the emperor's training exercise?"

"I don't know what it is," Norlin said, looking over the sensor readings of the glowing plasma torus. He worked quickly on his computer and traced out a trajectory that vectored the Preceptor directly through the center of the ring. Without asking for Sarov to double-check his figures, he punched in the course.

The ship lurched then steadied, driving hard for the middle of the gas ring.

Norlin had plotted the course for them to reach the center in minimum time and maximize distance and energy for the two pursuing cruisers should they try to intercept. He hoped to buy a few extra minutes this way. Neither of the other ships had a commander crazy enough to blast through the gas ring to get to him.

"It's working," Chikako said with some astonishment when she saw the course Norlin had laid in. "One cruiser has veered off rather than go through the plasma. The other is altering course enough to come at us from behind."

"We can defend against an ass shot," said Sarov. "I'm already dropping out countermeasures. Their missiles will have to be damned good to avoid that much kinetic material."

Norlin sucked in his breath and held it as the *Preceptor* flashed through the ring. He didn't know what to expect. A crackle of electrical discharge? Sparks flying from his fingertips? Something even more dramatic?

Nothing at all happened. The ship simply passed from one side to the other.

"Captain, I'm picking up a com-link message to us from the space station in geosynch around Earth."

"That's Arian's recognition signal," gasped Trahnee. "The emperor himself is trying to contact us!"

"Let's talk to him," said Norlin, hardly believing the ruler of forty-eight planets was personally trying to communicate with him. Even if the emperor knew they had destroyed his flagship, he wouldn't deal with them himself.

"Congratulations!" Emperor Arian's face filled the *Preceptor's* vidscreen. Norlin recoiled at the image. The face was a hundred times life-size. He tried to scale down the vidscreen display and failed. Arian wanted to appear larger than life, and the complex incoming signal auto-jammed any attempt to scale it down.

"Your Imperial Majesty?"

"Of course, my heroes. You have won the games! You have defeated the best in the Empire Service. You are the victors and deserve my fullest recognition."

"We will have an audience with him," murmured Trahnee. "Do not mention me, Pier. I beg you!"

Norlin waved her to silence.

"I don't understand, Majesty. What was the plasma ring?"

"The finish line, of course. You were the first through and are therefore the grand winners! Not that you wouldn't be honored for defeating those fools aboard the *Negation*."

"Your flagship?"

"Of course it was my flagship. What are you, brain dead?" The snappish response startled Norlin. For the first time he realized he really spoke to Emperor Arian and not an underling.

"We have information that must be presented to you personally, Majesty. It has bearing on the survival of the empire."

"None of that space dust, Commander. What is your ship? I thought I knew all my vessels taking part. I followed the favorites in my computer, but you just slipped in, it seems."

"Sir, this is the Nova Class Cruiser *Preceptor*, Sub-commander Pier Norlin at the helm."

"You're not on the list. Has Tidzio called in a ringer? That old devil. He's brought in a ringer from the colonies! The scoundrel!"

"Majesty, I must present my information to you directly concerning the Kindarian threat."

"What?" Emperor Arian looked genuinely surprised. "I don't understand you."

"The Kindarian Death Fleet. The aliens who have destroyed no fewer than ten colony worlds so far. We have proof that they are preparing to attack Alpha Centauri. We—"

"Silence! This *is* a joke. Chamberlain Tidzio put you up to it. I'll have his tongue cut out for this. Yours, too."

"An audience," whispered Trahnee. "Get the audience. Don't bait him now. He's in a poor mood."

"I see that," Norlin said in an aside. Louder, to Emperor Arian he said, "I beg forgiveness, Majesty. The thrill of such an immense victory has left me...witless."

"I noticed," the emperor sniffed. "Do come ahead. You will be given all courtesy at Star's End. Enjoy yourself briefly, then present yourself at the foot of the Crystal Throne for your reward."

The huge head vanished from the vidscreen. The abrupt disappearance caused Norlin to blink in dismay. He wasn't certain he had seen and heard all that he had.

"Star's End is the space station in the geosynchronous orbit," said Chikako. "I just received our clearance."

"Contact them and get dry dock facilities working on our damage. I want everything shipshape when we get back from seeing the emperor." Norlin reached out and took Trahnee's hand. She looked apprehensive at the idea of returning to Emperor Arian's court.

Norlin turned the controls over to Liottey, letting the first officer guide the *Preceptor* into the docking bay indicated by the space station's controller.

"We can't stay on Star's End long," he told Trahnee. "How do we get a shuttle to the emperor's court?"

"Do not be in such a hurry to stand before Arian. You have won his exercise and are his current darling. Whim will place someone else in that position too soon."

"All the more reason to get to the Crystal Throne as quickly as we can. I *have* to present the facts about the Death Fleet and what we've learned about the Black Nebula." He touched the com-link at his belt and got Barse.

"The prisoner," he asked. "How did he fare during the battle?"

"The vidcams are gone, Cap'n," came Barse's immediate answer. "But the little bastard came through the fight just fine. Better'n we did, if you ask me."

"I'm not asking. Prepare him for shuttling down to the emperor's court. Let Liottey handle it. I want you to oversee repair."

"I've already begun, Cap'n. They've got one fine setup here. There won't be any trouble getting what we need. I might not even have to threaten anyone to get it, either."

"Good."

Norlin looked at Trahnee and started to speak. The airlock cycled open, and he got his first look at Emperor Arian's space station, so aptly called Star's End. Words failed him.

# Chapter Six

"Welcome, conquering heroes!"

Music blared, and rows of ribboned and be-medaled officers snapped to attention, giving Norlin and Trahnee a salute so sharp it had knife edges on it. Norlin simply stood and stared until Trahnee nudged him.

"Go on. You're the hero of the moment. Make of it what you can. It won't last."

The bitterness in her voice bothered him. She wasn't using her genhanced ability to influence him. This was true emotion on her part—and he was interpreting it the way he wanted. She had lived with these people and knew their ways. They might be human, but they weren't Norlin's kind. He wished he were back on the frontier. The people there lacked the sophistication and polish so obvious here, but he was more comfortable with that. He couldn't help believing duplicity lay under this show of respect.

"Captain Norlin, I believe?" A tall woman who seemed to be wearing woven electricity glided rather than walked over to him. She threw her arms around his neck and kissed him. Norlin accepted this greeting in spite of Trahnee's sniff of disapproval. "How wonderful that you've won Emperor Arian's maneuvers. You are a champion." In a lower voice, the two-meter tall, statuesque woman added, "And I would like to be yours this night."

The words had barely come from her violet-tinted lips when another, even more beautiful woman pushed her aside.

"Me, take me!"

"No, me!" The chorus went up, men joining it also until Norlin silenced them with a shout.

"Stop! Thank you, one and all." His eyes roved back to the tall woman dressed in the ever-changing sheath of blue-and-white electricity. The discharges revealed large patches of skin, though he could not call her naked. Certain parts were always—almost—hidden behind the shifting cloak of translucent energy.

"Your crew is to be given the fullest courtesy," the tall woman said, obviously appointing herself as his shepherd. She moved with an easy grace to interpose herself between him and Trahnee.

The corona of the woman's garment brushed his arm. The surge he felt did more than tingle. It stimulated him. In every way. He looked to Trahnee for help. She shot him a disgusted look and let the crowd move between them. She was not the hero of the day. She hadn't defeated the emperor's own flagship in combat. He had to bear the brunt of the publicity and notoriety.

"My crew," he stammered out. "I need to see to them. I need to get the *Preceptor* repaired."

"Do not worry about such things. It is time for rejoicing. For festivity. For garnering your well-earned reward," the woman said.

Her long fingers stroked up and down his arm. The lightest nick of her purple-lacquered nails sent his heart racing. He recognized the effect of a genetically engineered aphrodisiac drug but could not fight it. The milligram that had entered his bloodstream thrilled him a thousand times more than the electric brush of the woman's raiment.

The crowd cheered and carried him along. He found himself on a small platform, dozens of vidcams focused on him. The woman who had appointed herself his guardian nipped at his earlobe as she whispered, "Do your duty."

"What?" He turned and stared at her, startled. "What do you mean?"

"The emperor's public. They want a speech. Give them a rousing speech. You are com-linked across Earth."

Norlin stared ahead at the compound PLZT ceramic lenses of the electronic cameras. This was an opportunity he had not believed he would ever get. He could take the message of the Kindarian Death Fleet directly to the people of the Empire. Once alerted, they would rally and assemble the fleet needed to carve out the heart of the Black Nebula.

He started speaking but noticed the camera operators were not following him. He stopped suddenly, after telling of the destruction of several colony worlds and Admiral Bendo's successful defense at Sutton. He turned to the woman cloaked in the dancing veils of electrical gauze.

"The vidcams aren't tracking me. What's wrong?"

"Just move about and wave your arms. Of course they're not really 'casting you across the Earth. You're not genhanced. You don't know how to speak, and who'd want to hear what you said even if you did? Everything will be added later. They're just establishing a baseline for the computer imagining."

"I'm not getting my message to the people?" he asked, dumbfounded.

"No, you silly gust of solar wind. Only genhanced are allowed on the vids, and for good reason. Non-genhanced would just rouse the people needlessly." She sidled closer and ran her hands over him again. "Can I rouse you now?"

Before Norlin could answer, the vidcam crews vanished and the sea of people parted once more. A small man dressed in court robes slowly crossed the space opened before the platform.

Even the aggressive woman in her electrical garb fell back in deference to the newcomer. Norlin wasn't sure who this was. It couldn't be the emperor. Arian never left Earth, or so he'd heard.

"Congratulations on your destruction of the *Negation*. Admiral Hoog had become complacent and expected only easy victories. You give all the Empire Service fleet a lesson in tactics and preparedness. I salute you."

The man bowed slightly, giving Norlin a chance to compose himself. He was still upset that he had failed to get word to the people of Earth about the Kindarian threat.

The man before him was short, hardly more than a hundred-fifty centimeters tall. His skin was sallow, whether because of racial heritage or illness Norlin couldn't say. Deep wrinkles turned his face into something ancient and malign. The tiny lines at the corners of the mouth and the cruel set to the deeply sunken ebony eyes spoke more eloquently than the man ever could. This man wielded immense power—and did it maliciously.

Norlin tried to imagine the slight man as being genhanced and failed. Yet he commanded deference from those on Star's End who *were* genetically enhanced. Norlin decided to hide his confusion behind politeness and formality until he knew who he faced.

"You are too kind. All I do is in the name of Emperor Arian."

"Of course it is," the robed man said, a slight sneer on his thin lips. "A loyal officer to the death." The way he spoke told Norlin that more than one had died after being branded "loyal."

"My cruiser was damaged in the…exercise. I need it restored to full operation."

"Consider it done. The finest technicians on Star's End will repair your ship. What else can I do to make your stay here a welcome and joyous one?"

Norlin started to tell the man of the Kindarian threat when he saw Trahnee out of the corner of his eye. She shook her head vigorously, warning him to silence. His hesitation caused the robed man to swing around. The smile that lit his face was both evil and filled with genuine affection.

"Is this your current pet? I might have known. You always gravitated toward strength, just as a black hole sucks in everything worthwhile around it in space."

"Chamberlain Tidzio," she said, bowing deeply. "It is a true delight to see that you have not changed since Bo and I left for the colonies."

Only then did Norlin put the name with the title. Chamberlain Tidzio had driven Trahnee and Delamier from Earth. Trahnee had called him the true power in the Empire, though Norlin wondered how this might be. Such a homunculus lacked the physical presence to command effectively. Chamberlain

Tidzio might be brilliant but who would follow this wizened old man to the death?

"How is your dear brother?" Tidzio asked.

Norlin heard the ripple of hatred in that question. When Trahnee told him of Bo Delamier's death, the response was one of amusement.

"He lived to the fullest. There is no reason he should not have perished in the same way," Tidzio said. The small man turned back to Norlin. "You will meet with the emperor in one day. He is anxious to meet the commander who destroyed his favorite ship."

"I…"

"We will accept the honor of an audience with Emperor Arian," Trahnee cut in. Norlin heard the vibrant tones she used, soothing and reassuring Tidzio.

"I will arrange for the audience with our august emperor," Tidzio said.

"Let us discuss this in more detail," Trahnee said, adding an air of urgency to her words. Norlin wanted to discuss it; the force of the genhanced woman's words worked their magic on him. Tidzio seemed immune from her gentle suasion.

"Let us discuss it over a cup of chocolate. There is nothing quite like it in the universe, is there, my darling Trahnee?" Tidzio motioned, and the crowd parted. Chamberlain and genhanced lady walked off arm-in-arm, chatting like old friends instead of bitter rivals.

"My name is Gianina," the tall woman said, again at Norlin's side before the others could return. "Allow me to show you the pleasures of Star's End."

"Very well," Norlin said, distracted. He watched Tidzio and Trahnee vanish down a broad corridor, worried about the deals that might be struck between them. Trahnee had returned to the center of power in the empire. She knew the politics of the emperor's court. What might she trade for a return to grace before the Crystal Throne?

"You seem occupied with our chamberlain," Gianina said. "He is such a dear old man, even if he does have such a silly name."

"Silly?"

"He is Chinese—or from the province that used to be China. I don't remember where that is. Somewhere down there," she said making a vague gesture with her long-fingered hand. The light reflected off the lacquered nails almost blinded him. "Rumor has it the name means pig piss."

"What's that?" Norlin asked, startled. He turned his full attention to Gianina, which was what she had sought.

"The story goes that the old Chinese gods—before they had a true emperor—came down and stole baby boys. Only those who were unattractive or revolting escaped their kidnaping. Vile names were often given to drive away the gods." Gianina tittered. "They didn't have to name *him* Pig Piss. Any god looking at him would have been frightened away. He *is* ugly, don't you think?"

"But powerful," Norlin said. "He has the emperor's ear."

"Most likely," the woman agreed. "He might even carry it on a string around his neck. Tidzio is often…frolicsome."

"I must tend to my ship," he said, trying to pull away.

Again Gianina nicked him with her nails, and the aphrodisiac drug flooded his system. Try as he might, Norlin could not leave her. Gianina had captured him and held him firmly in chemical thrall.

"Allow me to show you the joys Star's End has to offer. No other place in the galaxy has as many diversions. Not even Porlock Five."

"I was just there," Norlin said.

"Tell me about it! You must *show* me how it compares to all that is offered freely here, to a conquering hero, to a man who can have anything he wants."

She rubbed against him. The combination of her drug and the electrical discharge from her gown pulled him along beside her like a captive satellite.

Norlin found himself forgetting about repair work on the *Preceptor* and thinking more about his surroundings. Even Porlock had not offered such diversions. Gianina insisted that they stop in several restaurants along the wide corridor teeming with people in all modes of dress and undress. Each restaurant put a single dish before them. Gianina explained the history and preparation of the dish with gusto before urging him to help her devour it.

The subtle tastes blended and flowed across his tongue. He felt giddy and alert at the same time. His senses became more acute—and he became more aware of Gianina with every passing minute.

"A night of sampling is not enough, not for you," the woman insisted. She paraded around in front of the throngs wanting to see the captain of the ship that had destroyed the midget battleship *Negation*. Gianina basked in the adoration as much as Norlin.

He had never cared for such public acclaim. Now he thrived on it, blossoming like a bud kept too long in the dark. It might have been the food laced with exotic drugs, it might have been Gianina's presence, it might have been a combination of everything. Pier Norlin began to revel in the acclaim he received.

It was almost a shame that he would have to leave this to seek out the Kindarian homeworld in the Black Nebula. The threat to humanity had not passed because he had become popular and even renowned. But for the moment, he would accept all that Star's End had to offer and not think of the task that lay before him.

"She is lovely," Gianina said. "Is she your woman?"

"Who? Trahnee?" Norlin said almost guiltily. It had been hours since he'd thought of her. "You make it sound as if she's property and belongs to me. It's not like that."

"Good," said Gianina. She took his hand and tugged him toward a cacophonous, brightly lit room off the main corridor. "This is my favorite spot in all Star's End. See if you don't agree with me."

They entered the room. At first Norlin thought they were alone in a forest. Then he saw that he had walked into a giant vidscreen. Holograms flickered on and off in all directions. One spot showed high mountains. Another a crowded city. In still another direction he saw the limitless depths of stars. From all directions came sounds that assaulted his ears.

"That's a real view," Gianina said. "It never changes. The others can be altered to your mood, changed at random or even specifically chosen for artistic effect. Come along, Pier. Let's find just the right place."

Norlin let her lead him through the maze of feathery ferns, both real and projected. They came out on a savanna. His hand flashed to his laser pistol when a lion snarled and started to pounce. The creature hunkered down then launched itself in a display of blinding speed that took it past—through!—him and toward a distant herd of gazelle he had not seen behind him.

Gianina laughed gleefully.

"Isn't it wonderful!" she cried. "It is so real you feel as if you were in Africa."

"Africa? That's where this place really exists?" He had never heard of Africa but decided to avoid it. The lion had caught a slow-moving gazelle and ripped its haunch off in bloody gobbets. Its table manners were less than polite as it began its raw meal.

"There's more. Come, come along!" Gianina tugged at his hand and led him across the veldt to a forested area. Under the starry band of the Milky Way stretching across the sky, a fountain of water tumbled down a rocky slope. The grass was softer than any velvet Norlin had ever felt.

"Isn't this better?" Gianina asked. She looked into his eyes. Her lips parted slightly. He felt the nick of her drug-laden nails. He kissed her.

The world swung in a wildly eccentric orbit around him. He sank down to the grassy sward, aware that Gianina remained standing. She looked down at him, an almost shy smile dancing at the corners of her full, purple-tinted lips.

"I'm glad you defeated the *Negation*," she said. "Admiral Hoog was such a null. You excite me."

She reached under the shifting blue-and-white sparks of her dress and touched a switch. The display crackled and died, leaving behind only a few wires and the woman's sleek, naked flesh.

"Lovely," Norlin said. He fought the effect of the drugs then surrendered totally. They were too cunning. They raced through his bloodstream and caused reactions he could not control.

"Don't think of her," Gianina said. "She and Tidzio are talking politics. I know. That's all he ever talks of. The man is a eunuch. He won't harm your woman."

"Trahnee?" Norlin was almost paralyzed with lust now. His breath came in short, fast gasps, and fever caused sweat to bead on his forehead. His uniform had become too tight. He couldn't get it off quickly enough to suit him—or Gianina.

Her fingers slid across his bare skin, teasing and tormenting. "So nice. Such muscles."

Norlin sank supine to the grassy surface, looking past the woman to the waterfall, the verdant undergrowth, the black band dotted with crystalline stars above. Everything was perfect. She stepped over him, straddled him, knelt over his groin. Never had he believed himself capable of such passion.

Locked in the woman's arms as she bent forward, Norlin tried to discount the sensation of being watched. They were in a room filled with hundreds—thousands—of others separated only by clever holographic imaging. There had to be sounds. When they had entered, he thought they were coming into a nightclub.

The sensation of being spied on grew even as the power in his loins mounted.

Norlin struggled under Gianina, thrashing about. He reached out and found his discarded uniform. As he sought his belt and the laser pistol holstered there, a heavy boot crushed down on his wrist. He looked up and into the massive dark maw of a projectile weapon.

# Chapter Seven

"Die, traitor," the man with the projectile weapon said.

Norlin was pinned down by Gianina's naked weight. The woman stirred, still fogged by her own desires. She didn't know what was happening. Norlin twisted his arm to the side and pulled his hand back, getting his wrist free of the man's imprisoning boot sole.

The weapon in the man's hand spat the heat-seeking projectile at the same instant Norlin jerked away. Gianina screamed and moved—and drew the projectile a fraction of a millimeter in her direction. A look of surprise, agony and utter incomprehension crossed her lovely face.

She opened her mouth to scream again. Blood erupted in a fiery geyser, the small missile already rooting about in her guts.

Norlin took this in and knew his life would be forfeit if the assassin fired a second time. He didn't try to retrieve his own weapon. He rolled to the side and kept rolling until he plunged under the churning hologram of the waterfall.

He found himself naked and in the presence of a sedate party of elderly revelers.

"Sorry," he said.

They looked at him with some distaste but said nothing. They lived on Star's End. They knew the type of carousing that went on in places such as this.

Norlin ran, expecting the heat-seeking missile to lock onto his thermal signature and kill him at any instant. He dodged to the side and dived parallel to the floor. He hit hard, skidding along past several others who never noticed him. They were too engrossed in one another to notice anything less than the projectile exploding in their faces.

Breathing hard, he wiggled forward and came up against something solid in the phantom paradise of holo images. He looked up and saw a disapproving man frowning at him.

"There's someone after me. He killed the woman I was with. Get the authorities!"

"You disgust me," the man said. He spat at Norlin. "You let your fantasies intrude on everyone else. I hope you do die in your fabrication."

"This is *real*. I'm Pier Norlin. I just—" Norlin found himself talking to thin air. The man had pulled his small cart away and vanished into the damp white fog surrounding them.

Norlin stayed seated on the floor, waiting, watching, every sense strained to the utmost. He didn't wait long. The telltale hiss of a heat-seeker ripping through the air came to him. He looked around in vain for a way to decoy it. He saw nothing that would save him from the same excruciating death that had taken the woman.

The mist parted, and the blunt head of the projectile arrowed toward him. He tried to dodge at the last instant, although he knew such movement wasn't likely to save his life. Tiny steering jets on the sides of the projectile could move it faster than any human could react.

The explosion lifted him and threw him backward. He smashed hard into a wall, the breath knocked out of his lungs. Gasping for air, he wondered if he had died and this was hell. Heaven couldn't hold this much pain.

His vision was blurred, but he saw two figures come through the holographic murk.

"You all right, Cap'n?"

"Tia!"

"Who else?" his engineer asked in disgust. "That bitch of yours is off with the mousy chamberlain agreeing to who knows what. Gowan and me came hunting for you. Just about in time,

I'd say." Barse stared at him, a smile wrinkling the corners of her mouth. "Is that Star's End's version of a formal uniform?"

"Here," offered Liottey. The first officer passed over his uniform jacket.

Norlin draped it around his waist and immediately felt better. Being naked took away dignity and robbed him of his composure.

"A weapon. Give me a weapon."

Barse unlimbered the laserifle she carried and handed it to him; she still clutched the laser pistol she had used to destroy the heat-seeker. He checked the charge. It was enough to burn the assassin who had killed Gianina and had almost murdered him.

"You wouldn't mind telling us what happened, would you, Cap'n? We came looking for you to report on the *Preceptor*'s status. It's going well."

"The repair?" Norlin had other matters on his mind. Somewhere in the shifting mirage of the holographic recreation area, a man with a projectile pistol hunted him.

"What else? Look, Cap'n, if you want help tracking someone down, let us know. Gowan and I can do it. We're your officers."

"This is personal. What equipment did you bring with you?"

"Equipment?" Liottey and Barse exchanged glances. Barse shrugged. "Not much. I never go anywhere without the laserifle now—especially not in this den of iniquity. I've had more indecent proposals than I ever got the whole time I was knocking around on the frontier."

"She was thinking seriously about two of them," added Liottey.

"Space gas. "Don't listen to him." She smiled broadly. "One of them sounded interesting, though. I might just—"

"I've got a killer to track down. This is no game. Gowan, let me have your pistol, too. I want firepower."

"Sir, wait," the *Preceptor*'s first officer called when Norlin started back in the direction of the holographic waterfall where Gianina had died. "Do you want any help?"

"Get Trahnee. Tell her someone's after me. They might want to harm her, too."

"That bitch is mixed up in politics again. That's what precipitated this," grumbled Barse.

"You're probably right. I didn't know the man who tried to burn me. He might be just a thrill-seeker, but I don't think so. There was something about him, like he was delivering a message from someone else."

"A professional killer?" ventured Liottey.

Norlin nodded.

"Sir, if you won't let us join you, let me give you these."

Liottey skinned out of his trousers and handed them to his captain. Norlin took them without comment. He passed the man's uniform jacket back, feeling as if he could outmatch any assassin sent against him now. Having pants on made the difference.

The laser pistol tucked into the waistband and the laserifle he carried at ready made an even bigger difference in the way he felt. No longer the hunted, he had turned into the hunter. And he wasn't going to stop until somebody paid with his life.

He stopped and looked back. Both Barse and Liottey had vanished. He decided it was for the best. He knew what the assassin looked like, and they didn't.

And he wanted vengeance.

A desert stretched unexpectedly in front of him. Joshua trees shivered in an unseen wind. When they began stalking toward him, he lifted the laserifle and waited. His finger curled back on the firing stud instinctively when he saw another heat-seeking projectile appear in front of an ersatz tree. The explosion knocked him to his knees; it brought the woman firing the weapon to the ground.

Norlin wasted no time getting to her side. She was burned and moaned softly. She opened her eyes and glared at him.

"You devil," she whispered. "We'll get you. There won't be atoms of you left when we get you!"

"Why are you trying to kill me?" asked Norlin, confused. "How many of you are there after me?"

"Enough to burn you, lap dog!"

The woman screamed in agony then slumped when a heat-seeking missile blew away the back of her head. Norlin crouched and swung up his laserifle, firing steadily. He knocked out two more of the deadly missiles.

He tried to locate the woman's killer and couldn't. The assassin's assassin had faded into the shifting quagmire of holographic images.

He hiked off into the false desert and soon found himself on a barren planetoid. The transition from desert to airless world took him by surprise. Involuntarily, he sucked in his breath; the illusion did not extend to robbing him of atmosphere.

He tried to scan every boulder and crater on the rocky surface as he tried to work through the maze of conflict around him.

The woman had known him; she had alluded to many assassins stalking him. Had she been killed by her own side accidentally, or was that their way of preventing her from revealing too much?

He had no way of knowing. He continued across the rocky surface that felt smooth under his bare feet. The illusion cast by the holographic projectors was almost perfect. Shadows appeared where they ought to, and he moved to avoid rocks that were insubstantial when he reached out to touch them.

He came to the outer wall of the holographic display. Moving with it to his back, he circled until he found the entrance. For several minutes, he did nothing but watch and wait.

His patience was rewarded—the man who had killed Gianina tried to slip out unobtrusively. Norlin thought about following him then discarded the idea. He knew nothing about Star's End. Once the man left the holo displays, he might lose him within a few meters in the crush of people outside.

Norlin let the man come even with where he stood, behind a substantial column holding the complex electronic circuitry responsible for projecting the images. Swinging the laserifle, he connected squarely with the side of the man's head.

The killer tumbled to the floor, but to Norlin's considerable astonishment, he wasn't knocked out. His reflexes were superbly tuned, and he jerked aside at the last possible instant to rob the blow of its full power.

Pier Norlin knew he faced a genhanced.

He swung the laserifle around and turned on the sighting spot. A red dot appeared in the middle of the fallen man's belly. Norlin didn't have to tell him the weapon fired where the red dot rested.

"You will die, traitor," the man snarled. "If I don't kill you, another will."

"Who are you? Why did you kill Gianina—and why do you want me dead?"

"Dupe! Pawn of the emperor!"

Norlin's finger touched the firing stud as the man moved to pull his projectile weapon. He wanted to question him further but knew he would be dead if he didn't respond quickly. This genhanced killer's reflexes were faster than his—but not by enough.

The laserifle roared. The assassin was reduced to a sizzling spot on the floor. Several men and women entering the holographic displays stopped, wrinkled their noses at the ugly smell of charred human flesh and left hurried away. They had no desire to be a part of such graphic recreations. Norlin didn't have time to tell them this was real life and death, not images from a computer-driven hologram projector.

He checked the dead man but found nothing to identify him. The few pockets untouched by the laser fire that had claimed the man's life disgorged nothing of interest.

Norlin stood, wondering what he should do. This was the only assassin he knew about, but the woman had tried to murder him, too. More than one killer had been loosed in the forests of imaginary night. How could he ever recognize others before they killed him?

He couldn't. The deadly drama had played out. All he could do was locate the spot where he had left Gianina and call the authorities to retrieve her body. He had no idea if she had family or, indeed, know anything about her. He didn't even know her last name.

Taking the fallen killer's projectile weapon, Norlin tucked it into his waistband. It made a heavy load to carry with Liottey's laser pistol beside it, but he wasn't going to leave weapons behind him. He might need it later—and he certainly didn't want someone picking it up and using it against him.

He made his way back through the shifting maze of holo images and finally located the waterfall where Gianina had been killed. It took another few minutes' searching before he found her body lying against a column. He looked at her corpse, then turned to the column and fiddled with it until the images winked off.

Only then did he kneel and check her. She was very dead. The projectile had been a miniature burrow-and-explode. It had rooted around inside her for several seconds before detonating. Very little of her innards were intact, either because of the digging action or the explosion's shock wave.

Having the holographic images turned off saved his life. He knew the two moving in on him were real. The dark floor and walls caused them to vanish, since both were dressed in black, but he saw the glint of light off their projectile weapons. He opened fire on the nearest man before he could launch his heat-seeker.

The woman yelled incoherently and fired.

Norlin was in a desperate fight to stay alive. The heat-seeking projectile had locked onto his thermal signature; swiveling his laserifle around didn't distract the small tracking computer in its warhead. He tossed the weapon aside and dived in the other direction just as a proximity fuse detonated the explosive. The powerful discharge ripped flesh away from his upper body. He felt the trousers he had donned beginning to smolder from fragments of the warhead. Worst of all, he was momentarily helpless and at the woman's mercy.

He doubted she had any mercy to spare, and her words hardened that doubt into certainty.

"You killed Frio, you space-sucking bastard!" she shrieked.

Another heat-seeker blasted toward him. The missile was slower than others owing to its complex homing device, but it was more certain than other types of guided seek-and-kills.

Norlin fumbled for the projectile weapon he had taken from the other assassin. He struggled to get it free; he couldn't. His finger tightened on the trigger, and he fired through the fabric of his trousers. Heat lashed his groin and seared flesh along his thigh.

The two missiles destroyed each other less than two meters in front of him. The concussion blew him flat to the floor and left him stunned. What it did to the woman he had no idea.

"Pier, are you all right?" came Trahnee's anxious words.

"Get her. She's armed, dangerous."

"Who? Who did you shoot at? You're on fire!"

Norlin felt the genhanced woman's hands trying to smother his burning trousers. He pushed her away. Concentrating on getting the fire out, he beat at the glowing embers threatening to burst into flames at any instant.

"You look a fright. You're bloody and burned and half-naked." She stared at him for a moment. An almost shy smile crept across her face. "I like that part."

"The woman," he insisted. "She tried to kill me. Where is she?"

"I saw no one."

Norlin pulled the laser pistol from his tattered waistband and pushed himself erect. The holographic projectors throughout the rest of the area winked off as power failed. The brief but fierce missile fight had damaged much of the circuitry around him.

"There!" he cried. "That's her!"

He had sighted his would-be killer running away. As if he stood on a target range, Norlin set his feet, lifted the laser pistol and fired. The energy beam caught the woman high in the right shoulder and sent her cartwheeling. He fired a second time and missed.

"I want her alive," he told Trahnee. "There is an entire squad of killers loose here—and they all want my blood."

The genhanced woman nodded briskly. She understood the importance of taking this prisoner. She kept pace with him as he dashed across the now-barren room, pushing confused patrons out of the way as he ran. He fired repeatedly when it became apparent the woman was trying to bring her projectile weapon up and train it on him. A chance beam melted the barrel. The woman tossed the useless weapon to one side and tried to escape.

"Stop!" barked Trahnee.

The single word froze the fleeing woman in her tracks. Like one under the influence of a mind-numbing drug, she turned and faced Trahnee.

"I will kill you," she said, her voice quivering with anger and hatred.

"Why?" Trahnee's question was quieter. "You do not want to escape. You want to tell us why you want to harm Captain Norlin."

"He is Emperor Arian's favorite. We strike a blow for liberation from the emperor if we kill his favorite."

"Wonderful," Norlin said, slumping. "I'm mixed up in palace intrigue, and I don't give a damn about it. I don't care who is emperor. All I want is—"

"Pier, be quiet!" Trahnee said sharply. To the woman, she said, "We want to be your friend. We are not supporters of Emperor Arian. Who are you?"

"The Front for the Liberation of Mankind," came the proud but meaningless answer.

"Who is your leader?"

The woman fought Trahnee's persuasive voice. She turned red in the face as she struggled between the compulsion to answer the genhanced's question and maintaining secrecy.

"Our leader's code name is Eagle."

"What is your Eagle's real name? Who do we enlist to aid us in *our* fight against the emperor?"

"He is—"

The woman stiffened then toppled face-forward onto the floor. A dark, seared area in the middle of her back showed where a deadly laser beam had robbed her of life.

Norlin whirled, his own laser pistol looking for a target. He held himself in check when he saw the emperor's small chamberlain. Tidzio indolently passed his energy weapon to an aide.

"Rebels," Tidzio said indifferently. "They are such vermin. Exterminating them is such a nuisance, don't you agree?"

Norlin said nothing. And for once, even Trahnee was silent.

# Chapter Eight

"Remove this disagreeable refuse," Chamberlain Tidzio ordered his aide. The man bobbed his head and touched a com-link at his belt. Norlin heard the immediate response.

Robots rolled down the corridor from behind Tidzio. In minutes, the woman's body was removed, leaving only a memory. The robots even scrubbed the deck to pristine condition.

"This is one of the more troublesome aspects of life on Star's End," Tidzio said, as if lecturing a university class. "Many of our citizens find that the boundaries between reality and illusion blur. Living out their fantasies can become…deadly."

"It certainly interrupted my enjoyment of all Star's End had to offer," Norlin said. "What about the woman they killed?"

Tidzio's plucked eyebrow arched.

"'They?' More than one beset you? Oh, dear, this is vexing. Tend to this, also," he ordered over his shoulder.

The aide's hand flashed back to the com-link. Norlin imagined dozens of janitor robots scrubbing away the blood where Gianina's innards were turned to mush.

"You've lost control of your realm, Chamberlain," Trahnee said. "Your intelligence network is usually more efficient than this."

"I know their leaders. I had not realized more than one of these terribly confused people stalked your lovely Captain Norlin." The chamberlain's dark eyes took in Norlin's height without revealing any emotion.

Try as he might, Pier Norlin could not guess the thoughts racing in the diminutive chamberlain's mind. Even the fashionable contempt he had read in the man's expression before was now completely hidden.

"I'd like to return to the *Preceptor* now," he said. "After one small item, that is."

"Oh?" Tidzio's carefully sculpted eyebrow arched again. "Isn't this unpleasant matter closed?"

"Gianina died. I want some justice for her death."

"Gianina? One of the Painted Women who lurk about the docking bays? Did she amuse you so very much, Captain?"

"She's dead. She gave her life to save mine," Norlin lied. The chamberlain's attitude angered him. To Tidzio, a woman's death meant nothing. Less than nothing.

"It seems the ultimate price has already been paid by her killer," Tidzio said. He clapped his hands then studied a small vidscreen held by his aide. "From the appearance of *this* body, someone used a laser pistol on him. A pistol not unlike the one you still hold, Captain Norlin. Perhaps we should compare the frequency signature of your laser to that of the one that caused such deadly damage?"

Norlin thrust the weapon into the band of his trousers. For the first time since going hunting for the assassins, he *felt* naked.

"My ship," he said, dropping the subject. Let Trahnee deal with plots and counterplots against Emperor Arian. All he wanted to do was rest—and to forget the sudden death that had come into this fairyland of holographic fantasy.

"By all means, dear Captain Norlin. Allow me to lend you the invaluable assistance of my aide. He will guide you back to your fine ship. I am sure you'll find the repairs progressing nicely." Tidzio smiled. It wasn't a pleasant sight. "The royal shuttle will pick up you and your crew for the audience with the emperor early tomorrow morning. He who sits on the Crystal Throne is not inclined to smile when he is kept waiting. Be warned and act accordingly."

Chamberlain Tidzio spun and walked off. Norlin's hand twitched, and he reached for the laser pistol. Only Trahnee's restraining hand atop his kept him from reducing Tidzio to a cinder.

"It's not that easy, Pier," the genhanced woman said softly. "Star's End is his to use as he pleases. He is invincible in these corridors."

"He didn't know about Gianina's death—or the other killers'."

"A trivial matter. There is little else Tidzio does not know—when he has to. Let's return to the *Preceptor* and rest. He is correct that Arian becomes upset when he's kept waiting. Even someone who bested his flagship isn't immune to his wrath."

Norlin said nothing. The more he heard about the emperor, the more the man sounded like a petulant child. If people like Tidzio held the true reins of power, overturning the empire might not be such a bad idea.

Arm in arm, he and Trahnee returned to the ship. He conducted a quick inspection and found the royal chamberlain had not lied about the state of his cruiser. Repair was going swiftly and well. Only a few days' more work remained to return the *Preceptor* to her former peak condition. More to his liking, Barse had prevented the repair crew from examining the Kindarian radiation cannon, passing off the weapon as a small frontier modification and nothing more.

Satisfied with this aspect of their stay on Star's End, he and Trahnee retired for the night. As he fell asleep in her arms, he was thinking of dead Gianina.

✳ ✳ ✳

"I don't want to go down there," grumbled Tia Barse. "There's still work to be done on the *Preceptor*. I don't trust them to do it right. These station techs don't know how to balance a shift engine properly. We'll—"

"We'll all go because Emperor Arian commands it," Norlin said tiredly. He had slept poorly, images of a dying Gianina haunting his dreams. Trahnee sensed his discomfort and reached to touch his hand. He almost pulled away. He was drowning in her world and didn't like it.

What he didn't like most was being dependent on her to guide him through the morass of customs and ritual involved in meeting the emperor. He belonged in space; he sympathized with Barse more than he allowed himself to show openly and silently balanced continuing in the Empire Service with joining the frontier rebels.

All that held him back from turning rogue was the threat posed by the invaders from the Black Nebula. Only the full force of the empire could turn that deadly tide.

"I'm not sure it's a good idea leaving the *Preceptor* unguarded," said Gowan Liottey. This startled Norlin.

"What choice do we have? This is the center of the empire. Those are all top ES techs working on the ship."

"Will the biolock Barse put on the cannon be adequate to keep them from examining it?"

"If we catch a bit of luck, it will be."

Liottey shrugged. The changes caused by the brain damage were as startling as they were beneficial. He spent a good deal of his time studying. He still lacked Norlin's breadth of knowledge about the *Preceptor*, but he was focused on doing his job, which he had never been before.

Sarov and Miza stood huddled together, whispering so low Norlin couldn't hear them; he knew they were expressing similar reservations about meeting Emperor Arian. He took a deep breath and motioned for them to enter the royal shuttle. Rather than feeling honored, he had the sinking sensation they went to their deaths.

The acceleration cushions in the shuttle were posh. He also noted they did little to dampen the force of acceleration. The liftoff from Star's End was gentle, as if the pilot protected infirm passengers rather than highly trained and an experienced ES crew. Norlin sighed and leaned back, aware of Trahnee's arm pressing against his. They had to speak with the emperor. Nothing else mattered but driving a knife through the heart of the Kindarian realm.

"He will agree, won't he?" Norlin asked her.

She shrugged, knowing of his preoccupation.

The shuttle landed four hours later, after taking a leisurely spin around Earth. Norlin and his crew disembarked. For a moment, he thought the pilot had made a mistake.

---

The landing field shone with gems and precious metals. Everywhere he looked the ground was plated with gold.

"Emperor Arian has a flair for decoration," Trahnee said sarcastically. "Wait until you see the Crystal Throne. This is the low-rent district by comparison."

"No minimum-wagers here," Norlin muttered.

A tenth of the money spent plating the ground and buildings with gold leaf would have financed a major expedition against the Kindarians. He could chase them from the Black Nebula all the way to Andromeda for a fraction of the value of the gems studding doors and vehicles.

"This way, please," an obsequious driver said, motioning them toward a low-slung, bullet-shaped three-wheeled vehicle gleaming like ebony in the bright sunlight. Norlin and the others entered. The driver took them on a wild ride far more adventurous than the shuttle ride down from Star's End.

The black vehicle came to a smooth halt, and the doors popped open.

"Ah, you have arrived safely—and on time. That is good. The emperor awaits you," said Chamberlain Tidzio, standing on a small platform that added almost half a meter to his height. Even so, the chamberlain was hardly taller than Norlin or Sarov.

Tidzio shook free the voluminous folds in his elegant wine-colored robes and swung around. The soft swish of the fabric reminded Norlin of a woman's movement on the dance floor rather than a dynamic man going to meet his superior.

He did not make the mistake of underestimating Tidzio, however. He had seen the control the man exerted over Star's End. It must extend to Earth and the emperor's court. Norlin wasn't sure what the duties of a chamberlain were, but Tidzio displayed the arrogance of total power he had seen in the genhanced officers that had come to the frontier. Other than this arrogance, though, he had no evidence of the dwarf chamberlain's being genetically enhanced in any way.

The halls Tidzio led them down were even more opulent than the landing field. Paintings, statues, freeze-dried humans in various poses, even living sculpture adorned them. Norlin almost stumbled as he stared at one tableau. The golden people in it were alive and in extreme pain.

"The Rape of the Sabine Women," Tidzio said, not even glancing back. He had anticipated Norlin's reaction. "It is a reconstruction of a painting by someone or other."

"Nicholas Poussin," Trahnee said. "You should see the living reproduction of Jean Auguste Ingres' *Death of Socrates*. The poor bastard in it dies daily."

"Not so," said Tidzio, not even breaking stride. "It often takes a week or more before we have to provide the sculpture with a new participant."

"You *kill* the people in the living sculptures?" Norlin couldn't take his eyes off the graphic rape diorama. No one, Roman or Sabine, was enjoying a participatory role in the artwork.

"It is a great honor for them to take part in the emperor's art galley. This way. Do not look at Emperor Arian until he speaks to you. This is most important court courtesy. To violate the rule means instant death."

Norlin stopped in front of gigantic ten-meter-high doors that reflected all the colors of the rainbow.

"They look like diamond," he muttered.

Trahnee said, "They are. Each weighs almost a thousand kilograms. Single crystal, perfectly balanced, cut and mounted. They took eight years to create." She took his hand and squeezed it, then released it as the doors opened on their jeweled hinges.

The simple inlaid wood flooring leading to the Crystal Throne was deceptively plain after the ostentation in the rest of the emperor's palace. He discovered even this was remarkable, however, as he started his slow progress toward the distant throne. Every footstep caused the floor to chirp like a captive bird.

Norlin forced himself to only look at the floor as he marched ahead stolidly. He tried not to freeze in the presence of such power and awesome authority.

His thoughts wandered as he approached the throne of the emperor of all human-colonized space. The musical response of the floor began to irritate him. It was as if Emperor Arian had planned it this way. Peasants were allowed to stare only at the simple floor, listening to sounds they caused, not partaking of the true richness reserved for royalty—the genhanced.

Norlin was about to raise his head in anger to glare at the emperor when Arian spoke.

"My conquering heroes. Welcome to the foot of the Crystal Throne!"

Norlin and the others stared up the thirteen steps leading to the throne carved from a single ruby. Each of the steps blazed with a distinct color; each was constructed of a different precious gemstone. The light glowed softly from some, harshly from others. Somehow, the rays reflected back and focused on the occupant of the Crystal Throne, bathing him in a lambency that elevated him above mere humanity.

Pier Norlin almost laughed and demand to see the true emperor. The wizened man who sat on the Crystal Throne was not the one whose pictures he had seen all his life. He held his tongue when he saw the fierce light burning in Emperor Arian's eyes. The body might be twisted and small, but the mind seethed with vitality.

Demented vitality.

Like so many other genhanced, this man had passed beyond the bounds of sanity and embraced the darkness of mental aberration.

"We are honored to serve so great an emperor," Trahnee said, speaking for them.

Arian cocked his head to one side and fixed his hot gaze on her.

"You are a member of the *Preceptor*'s crew? You and your brother were exiled to somewhere or other."

"My brother is dead in the service of the empire," Trahnee said. "Captain Norlin has permitted me to travel with the *Preceptor*. I am not technically a member of the crew."

"Your Majesty," Norlin cut in, not wanting Trahnee to become embroiled in a power struggle with the emperor. "I bring a message of extreme urgency for your attention."

"Later," Emperor Arian said, his thin hand waving off Norlin's attempt to bring up the Kindarian threat. "You and you will dine with me. It is a great honor."

He had indicated Norlin and Trahnee. Norlin looked at his other four officers. Already servants led them away. Barse's face clouded with anger. He touched his com-link and told her on a private circuit, "Go along with them. Return to the *Preceptor*, if you can. See that everything is in prime condition. We'll be back when we can."

"Cap'n, this is outrageous!"

"Do it," Norlin said.

Emperor Arian had risen and danced down the thirteen steps leading to his glowing throne. He took both Trahnee and Norlin by the arm. The top of his head barely reached Norlin's shoulder. The young officer saw now why Arian had chosen Tidzio for his chamberlain. Few in the Empire Service would be shorter than the emperor.

"Let us go to a state banquet in your honor. Or someone's honor. It matters little to me. I do so enjoy receiving the winners of my training maneuvers. It makes me feel in touch with the officers who defend the empire."

Norlin saw Trahnee's sudden tension and wondered at its cause. He glanced around but didn't find Tidzio. The chamberlain would produce such anxiety, but a simple dinner hardly struck him as cause for alarm.

"There, there, you sit on my left and right. Positions of honor. Yes, oh, yes, you will enjoy this little fete."

Norlin looked down the long, elegantly set table. Ancient china dishes and fine crystal goblets were set before each guest. He stopped counting when he got to twenty on each side of the table. There might be as many as fifty people dining with the emperor—and he and Trahnee were at the ruler's elbows.

"Frolic!" cried Emperor Arian. "Drink. The wine is excellent. The finest from the vineyards of Earth and the colonies. My sommelier travels widely to find the best wines, no matter where they might spring up."

Arian delicately sampled the wine poured by the resplendently uniformed wine steward. Norlin sampled his, then drank more deeply. The wine combined hints of cinnamon and something more he could not quite identify. It pleased him, and he told the emperor.

"Excellent!" the ruler crowed. "My little hero likes the wine. You'll love the meal."

Silence fell along the table. All eyes turned to the emperor. He basked in their sudden attention. He stood and put his hands on the table, leaning forward slightly.

"One meal served this night is poisoned. A very subtle poison it is, but quite deadly. The effects are always fatal, and the death is lingering and exquisitely painful. Bon appetit!"

"It's poisoned?" Norlin stared at the food being served him. "Why should any of us eat it if one serving is poisoned?"

"Because, my dear little hero, if you don't eat every last morsel, the guards will kill you where you sit."

Norlin jerked around. Along the gallery stood dozens of Empire Service soldiers, each with a laser rifle aimed at a diner. He found the soldier covering him and saw no flicker of remorse in the man's eyes. He would shoot if Norlin didn't eat what might be a deadly meal.

"Only one is dangerous, Captain Norlin," the emperor said. "Your chances are quite good that it will be someone else's fate to dine unwisely this night." Emperor Arian laughed uproariously at his distress. "Why, it might even be *my* food! Yes, yes, even mine. I play fair, otherwise, the recreation is tedious."

The emperor ate quickly, smacking his lips and belching loudly. Norlin ate more slowly, acutely aware of the weapon trained on him. Trahnee sat across from him, her face strained and pale. The others at the table tried to make small talk, but the effort fell short of true affability.

"Why are you doing this?" Norlin asked.

"Why? For sport, Captain. It gets so dreary at court. No one knows how to enjoy themselves anymore. I do what I can to enliven these horrid state banquets. Who do you think will die? Her? No, not dear Trahnee. She is a lucky one. Her presence after being exiled shows that. Perhaps the lovely lady to your left? Her dinner companion? Or that ugly, festering sore of a man down there? Who? Who knows? No one! That is the life of the jest."

Norlin's belly grumbled when he had finished every crumb on the plate. He found himself taking a morbid interest in who had received the poison. None of his fellow diners appeared afflicted.

Emperor Arian finished his dessert and wiped his mouth, throwing the silk napkin onto the floor. A silent servant retrieved it and returned to stand behind his ruler, waiting for his next duty. Norlin tried to read something into the servants' attitudes and failed. They served and kept their thoughts to themselves.

"A fine meal. Congratulations to the chef," declared Arian. "Let us repair to a more informal setting and enjoy some parlor games. I do so love it when a conquering hero comes to court to stimulate us with his wit and daring."

"There is a danger to the empire, Majesty. I—"

"Hush, dear Captain Norlin. There is no danger at all. No one has died. I just said that to give zest to the meal." Arian strutted off, motioning for everyone to follow.

Trahnee whispered, "It is not often this way. Sometimes more than one dies. I survived a banquet where fully half the people died hideously."

"Why does anyone put up with this?"

"You begin to understand why Bo and I were exiled. There are others with the intent of overthrowing this capricious fool."

"Eagle," he said, remembering the code name of the revolt's leader. "Who is Eagle?"

Trahnee shrugged. "Probably none of these people. A true leader would not risk himself in this way. But do not speak further. The walls have ears. Tidzio listens to everything. I speak from experience."

"In here!" cried Emperor Arian. "Sit. Be comfortable. We will play the fragrance game. I am sure it is unlike anything you play on your warship, eh, Captain Norlin?"

"You are correct. I am unfamiliar with the game, Majesty."

The emperor waited for the dinner guests to settle themselves around the room. Pillows had been tossed onto the floor to afford comfortable seating. Small colored vials had been placed on low tables.

"It is a guessing game, one designed to test your sensual acuity. Take this vial, dear Captain, and inhale deeply."

The emperor held out an orange vial. He touched the button on the side. Norlin sniffed as the spray jetted up into his nostrils.

"What is it? Quick, now, identify the scent!"

"Rose?"

"Very good. My valiant space captain shows he has an aesthetic side to his warlike nature. Now you, Trahnee. Tell me what is in *this* vial."

Arian repeated the process. Norlin saw the way her nose wrinkled. She fought to keep from recoiling.

"Ah, she recognizes it. Yes, my dear, your shit does smell."

Norlin started to protest. Trahnee stopped him. The emperor worked his way around the room, giving everyone a preliminary sample of the game scents.

"He is protected by unseen guards," Trahnee said. "To even touch him spells your death."

"He can't be genhanced. There's no touch of genius in him. There's nothing but cruelty."

"At court, there is little distinction between the two, but you are wrong about one thing. Of the genhanced, Arian is the greatest."

The emperor finished his round and pointed to the tables.

"Take a vial. Open it, and the first to identify the scent wins a fabulous prize. Do it *now*!"

Norlin pressed the release on his and almost sneezed. He tried a second dose to see of he could identify the odor. Although not unpleasant, he did not like the scent and could not put a name to it.

Beside him, a woman dressed in a flowing natural silk gown stiffened, turned cyanotic and fell back in her pillow. She let out one shuddering gasp and died.

"She's dead!" Norlin cried.

"Very good! The captain lives up to his reputation. He is the first to identify a scent—death!" Emperor Arian clapped his hands. A servant entered with a large silver tray. On it lay an ancient sword in its sheath.

"Your prize, Captain Norlin—a samurai sword more than two millennia old. It is a priceless relic and still as useful as the day when master metallurgist and weapons master Yoritomo fashioned it."

Arian took the sheathed blade and passed it to the stunned Norlin.

"But what are you going to do about her?" He pointed to the dead woman. Her face had mottled in death. Ugly purple splotches marred her once perfect beauty.

"I usually leave them around as a reminder of victory—and defeat." The emperor scowled, then gestured. "Remove her. It is the captain's wish, and he is our honored guest this night. The first round goes to our dear cruiser commander. Prepare for the second!"

Norlin sat amid the comfort of the overstuffed pillows, feeling nothing. The ease with which death came at Emperor Arian's court appalled him.

He took another cylinder and sniffed at it warily. He recoiled. Icy needles drove far into his nose and brain. A moment of giddiness passed and gave him a visual clarity he had never experienced before. Every thought he had showed razor edges. His intelligence magnified, and his strength tripled. There was nothing he couldn't do.

He shook off Trahnee's restraining hand as he launched into pleading his case for invading the Black Nebula. He told Emperor Arian of the Kindarian menace, of their prisoner and how they had devastated colony worlds. Never had he spoken with such eloquence and authority. Tears flowed when he spoke of dead worlds and dead loves, of lost friends and burning destruction brought by the aliens and their Death Fleet.

Norlin had no idea how long he spoke. Minutes, hours—it didn't matter. He poured his soul into his plea for Emperor Arian's support in destroying the Kindarians.

Exhausted, he flopped back to let the emperor give his verdict. Did the Empire Service fleet invade, or would the colony worlds—and Alpha Centauri and even Earth—have to fight the Kindarians on a planet-to-planet basis?

"Come along, Pier. The game is over." Trahnee prodded him. He stirred, unsure of what had happened.

"Where is he? The emperor?"

"He left an hour ago. You have spoken well, and many who heard have pledged their aid. They know your honesty, your ability. They will help against the aliens."

"But...Arian," Norlin protested. "Where is he?"

"Who knows? Gone. You chanced upon a vial of hallucinogenic gas. Each person responds differently to it. In your case, it took away your fear and hesitation."

"Will he help, or is the empire doomed?"

"I cannot say. No one can. If Arian heard, he will consider your case. *Our* case. Come along now, and let's go to bed. Our quarters are near."

Numb and confused, he allowed Trahnee to lead him to a sumptuous sleeping room. He hardly noticed the furnishings or other luxuries. He tried to remember what he had said and done. He couldn't. He wasn't even sure if the hallucinogenic gas had left his system.

Trahnee quickly fell into a deep sleep. He sat up, staring into the subtly perfumed darkness. He was too bewildered either to sleep or think clearly.

# Chapter Nine

rahnee slept peacefully as Norlin sat, the ancient sword he had won lying across his lap. He lost track of the passage of time, staring into the darkness of the extravagant chamber. It might have been an hour or more when he heard soft movement.

At first, he thought he'd imagined it. Then he knew he had not. The door opened a fraction of a centimeter and let in a thin sliver of subdued light from the corridor.

The door closed.

Norlin came fully erect in the chair, laid down the sword and reached for the more useful laser pistol usually holstered at his belt. He silently cursed when he remembered he hadn't been allowed to wear it in the presence of Emperor Arian. The weapon had been left aboard the *Preceptor*.

He sensed rather than heard movement across the floor. He was about to cry out to warn Trahnee when he saw the shimmer of an energy weapon starting its charging cycle.

Norlin held in the warning as he stood. He couldn't see the silent assassin clearly; only dim outlines flowed past, dark against dark. He frowned. The killer was small, smaller than either Emperor Arian or Tidzio. Was everyone on Earth a dwarf?

Trahnee murmured in her sleep and turned over. She reached out for him, and he wasn't there. She stirred, sitting up and sleepily calling, "Pier? Where are you?"

He launched himself directly at the glowing energy weapon, his strong arm crashing down to carry it off target. The searing discharge burned his left arm. His right circled around the would-be killer's body.

The force of his dive carried both the assassin and him hard to the carpeted floor. Norlin stayed on top, fighting the kicking, clawing assailant. He forced his left arm down hard to keep the weapon pinned to the floor. His right he used as a club to bludgeon.

"Pier!" cried Trahnee. "What's happening?"

"Got me another killer. This one tried to shoot us in our sleep."

The lights came up as Trahnee touched the switch beside the bed. The intensity grew slowly, giving his eyes time to adjust. If the lights had flared on, he would have thought he'd gone blind—or crazy.

His captive was a small, furry creature that looked more like a bear than a human. Hardly a meter in height, the bear creature had mobile ears, hands with opposable thumbs and a mouth filled with savage, needle-sharp teeth. Norlin shifted his weight and got the energy weapon away from the bear-being. He jumped back to avoid a ferocious snap that threatened to bite off his right hand.

"Move, and you're cinders on this fine rug," he told the creature. Eyes burning with intelligence and hatred glared at him.

"What are you doing?" demanded Trahnee, speaking directly to the bear creature. "Prothasians have never shown such belligerence toward us before."

"Do you know this…him?" Norlin frowned as he studied the creature more carefully.

His first impression had been of a wild animal. He hadn't seen the small belt laden with tools or the almost invisible sandals the Prothasian wore. These, along with the obvious thumbs and the intelligence in the face, told him that he dealt with one of the alien races humanity had encountered and conquered. He had never seen a Prothasian before but had heard well of them.

"I know *of* him," Trahnee said. "The emperor enjoys having them around as pets. He baits them, I'm afraid, and treats them horribly."

"You mean he doesn't treat them any different than he does his own kind."

"You are so bitter toward him?" asked the alien. "Do not understand this. You are his general. You lead the expedition to wipe us out. You will destroy my homeworld!"

"What are you talking about?" asked Norlin. He lowered the energy weapon, checked it and found the dissipator switch. It hissed and crackled, then powered down. He laid the weapon aside. He didn't think he would need it to deal with the Prothasian, should the bear-like creature prove contentious.

The alien rocked forward, his center of gravity close to the floor. His eyes danced as he studied Norlin and Trahnee.

"You joke. Humans enjoy cruel jokes."

"Neither of us is Emperor Arian." The tone Norlin used startled the Prothasian even more.

"You are his trusted esteemed general. You speak of him so?"

"What do you mean 'esteemed general?'" asked Norlin. "We blundered into the middle of a military exercise and only defended ourselves. His flagship got destroyed when it attacked us. *That* is what this 'conquering hero' accolade means."

"Know that already," the Prothasian said, brushing the words aside with a paw clawing at the air. "You are to general his assault on my homeworld. Destroy everything there. I heard it. Heard you."

"I asked him to launch a fleet against the Kindarians in the Black Nebula. Are you an ally of theirs?"

"I know nothing of them. Heard you speaking of aliens. Who else is there? Most of us are dead." The small creature's agitation grew. He bounced up and down, never quite leaving the floor but giving the impression he would spring into the air at any instant.

"We have proof of the Kindarian Death Fleet destroying *our* worlds. We have no reason to take the Empire Service fleet to your world and destroy it. What we're doing is self-defense."

"You damage my world. You imprison many of us. He brings us here for amusement."

The accusations cut Norlin deeply. He looked at Trahnee. She had sought Emperor Arian's overthrow and had been exiled because of it. If she hadn't been genhanced she might have died—or if her talent had been any less. He had never understood why Arian had not killed her and Bo Delamier out of hand. The emperor showed no hesitation to kill randomly. The dinner and the inhalation game following it proved that his sadism knew no limits.

"He does similar things to his own kind," he pointed out. "The frontier worlds are breaking away from the empire. In some ways, that is good."

"Pier, darling," Trahnee said softly. Her fingers dug into his arm, warning him.

Norlin knew no part of the palace went unobserved, but urgency drove him. Their time on Earth—the time *for* Earth's survival—ran out rapidly.

"Emperor Arian knows nothing about what is happening in other parts of his realm, except where to get the finest wines. But I still don't understand what you mean about me being his general."

"Wants you to lead expedition against aliens," said the Prothasian. "I heard. You agreed."

"You were with him for more than thirty minutes, Pier," said Trahnee. "I couldn't hear what was being said. You *might* have convinced him before he left."

"I was drugged," said Norlin. "I can't remember any of it." His head still buzzed with the hallucinogen. He tried to heed Trahnee's warning, but his inhibition remained muted.

The time spent with Arian had faded from his mind like a barely remembered dream. He recalled nothing of his meeting with the emperor—or of having been able to present his case against the Kindarians.

"You excited him with tales of warfare. He wants you to general fleet and kill aliens for his glory." The Prothasian stood with pudgy arms crossed on his chest, hiding a small yellow sunburst design in his fur.

"Until a few minutes ago, when I saw you, I had no idea what a Prothasian looked like," Norlin said. "I have no quarrel with you or your homeworld. My anger is at the Kindarians. They have killed billions of my people."

"Friends? Lovers?" asked the bear creature.

Norlin only nodded. A lump formed in his throat as he thought of those who had perished under the alien death fleet's merciless assaults.

"We do not wish to harm the Prothasians more than you have been hurt already," Trahnee said. Norlin felt the vibrancy in her voice. She turned the full power of her genhanced ability on the Prothasian. "You are against many of the things we oppose also when we speak with Emperor Arian."

"You are humans," the bear creature protested. Norlin heard the tiny quiver of doubt in the Prothasian's voice. Trahnee's skills persuaded even this small alien.

"We are not enemies," Trahnee said convincingly. "We can be friends, in time."

"You are different," the Prothasian said.

"We are friends. I am Trahnee. This is Pier."

The bear creature shuddered and said quickly, "Oloroun. I am Oloroun the Arbiter."

"We are pleased to be Oloroun the Arbiter's friends," Norlin said. He didn't know if he should offer his hand. The Prothasian decided the matter for him by thrusting out both his paws. Norlin laid his hands against them. This satisfied the alien.

"Will Oloroun help us against the Kindarian threat?" asked Trahnee.

The Prothasian stared at her, dark black button eyes blazing.

"Will you help us against emperor threat?"

Norlin swallowed, seeing Trahnee's warning look. He knew they must be under surveillance by the chamberlain, if not the emperor himself. To say anything that smacked of treason would be used against him.

"This is not the time or place to discuss such matters. We are friends. Friends aid one another," Norlin said, trying to skirt the issue but not antagonize the Prothasian.

Oloroun nodded briskly then ran his clawed paws through his shaggy head of brown hair. Norlin tried to decipher the meaning of this motion and failed. It could mean anything—or nothing. He wished he had read more about these aliens, but their conquest had been quick and brutal. Only the rapidity of their defeat had saved them from massive destruction by the Empire

Service fleet, unlike the other two cultures discovered by humanity.

"Will show you horror," Oloroun said. He motioned with his paw.

Trahnee and Norlin exchanged glances.

"I will go. She must stay in case they come looking for us."

"I'll go, too," Trahnee said quickly. "They do not check that often." She smiled and stroked Oloroun's head. "After all, he has some freedom of motion inside the palace."

"I sneak well," Oloroun confided.

Norlin handed the energy weapon back to the Prothasian.

"Take this as a gesture of our mutual trust," he said.

He held his breath when Oloroun powered the weapon up and aimed it at him. The alien waited a moment then, satisfied about the integrity of his weapon, swung it away. Norlin and Trahnee followed as he peered out into the softly lit hallway.

The Prothasian darted out and vanished. Norlin and Trahnee found themselves hard-pressed to keep up as they tried to move without making any sound, keeping a vigil for guards and vidcams.

As they turned a corner, they entered a corridor and plunged into darkness.

"Why aren't there lights on?" Norlin muttered as he banged his shins against a low table. A vase rocked on its base. He almost reached out to grab it but held back. He might knock it over accidentally in the dark.

"Emperor Arian has odd ideas about security. He doesn't believe assassins can come upon him in the dark," answered Trahnee. "All the attempts so far *have* been made at night."

"I need a pair of IR goggles."

"Just follow Oloroun. His natural eyes are better than spectrum-enhancing devices," Trahnee said with more assurance than Norlin felt.

"Here," came the Prothasian's soft voice. "We go into this tight place and hide for minutes. Then we watch. Chamberlain makes all plans in here, and we see them."

Trahnee pressed tightly behind Norlin as they crowded into a narrow space. Norlin wanted to see what the entry looked like in bright light. He wondered if the small alien had stumbled across a secret passage in the heart of the emperor's palace. If so, others existed—and even more sophisticated devices abounded. Norlin suspected everyone spied on each other.

"Look," said Oloroun. "Here we see Tidzio. His name means pig piss."

"I heard," Norlin said, amused at the alien's bit of information.

He moved to a simple hole in the wall and pressed his eye against it. The other side of the hole had a fish-eye lens that gave a distorted view of the room but, since it used no power and was completely passive electronically, would be difficult to detect. All Norlin worried about was a heat signature detector inside the chamberlain's room directed at the walls.

He watched as Tidzio worked at a small terminal. By moving slightly, he saw over the chamberlain's shoulder and read what paraded across the screen. It took several seconds before he got the gist of the message.

"That son of a bitch!" he exclaimed as he pulled away from the wall. "He's put out an arrest order for Liottey and Barse."

"Why?" asked Oloroun. "You are emperor's pet general."

"The chamberlain is no friend of mine," said Trahnee. "This is blackmail to bind us to him. The emperor will send the fleet out to destroy the Kindarian homeworld, but Tidzio will force us to divert to another target."

"There are uprisings on four planets in the Plith Cluster. The worlds supply much of the material wealth Tidzio is diverting to his own coffers. Any disruption would hurt him financially."

"The Plith worlds have endured the brunt of Emperor Arian's anger for years. It isn't surprising they are ready to revolt." Trahnee let out a deep sigh. "If only Bo were alive. We could change the course of empire history."

Norlin didn't go into that. He knew Trahnee's ambition was to supplant the emperor, not change his policies. She loved him and he loved her, but her ambition still soared toward rule. His ambitions in the Empire Service were far less lofty but potentially as dangerous.

"What will you do?" asked Oloroun. "These people your friends?"

"Friends, yes, and even more important, they are vital crew members. I don't know how we'd keep the *Preceptor* functioning without them. Gowan isn't that much of a loss," Norlin mused, "but Barse is. She's the best shift engineer I've seen so far in the Empire Service. To go into battle without her would be almost suicidal."

"Tidzio chose well, then," said Oloroun. "I have looked to ways of killing him for years. There is none. He makes the guard around himself always very strong."

Norlin put his eye back to the spyhole and watched Tidzio as he worked on other, more arcane treacheries. As he observed the chamberlain, a plan began to form.

"Can we talk freely somewhere?" he asked. "Tidzio must have our sleeping chamber filled with a dozen different spy devices. We were lucky he was working on other schemes when Oloroun came in and missed what happened."

"My chamber is secure. I have many scrambler devices in place."

The reluctant tone the Prothasian used caused Trahnee to speak to him for several more minutes. Clearly, he was uncertain whether he should reveal his safe spot. Trahnee convinced him anew of their friendship.

They popped back into the hallway. Norlin and Trahnee blundered along for several hundred meters until a waist-high door opened and cast a pale yellow light into the corridor. Oloroun walked in. The two humans had to duck.

Once inside, they found they were in a high-technology bear den. Rough walls were hung with clever pieces of kinetic art. A shaggy carpet on the floor reminding Norlin of crushed grass was strewn with bits of electronic devices the Prothasian had torn apart.

Norlin and Trahnee sat cross-legged while Oloroun settled across from them.

"We are here safe. Scrambled images, replaced images," Oloroun assured them. He silently showed Norlin a device for intercepting Tidzio's signal and replacing it with an innocuous-appearing scene of a peacefully sleeping bear creature.

"We can't let the chamberlain take Barse and Liottey," Norlin said. "I have an idea how to stop it."

Bending forward, he motioned for Trahnee and Oloroun to put their heads close to his. They were safe within the bear cave, but this closeness added to his sense of security as they formulated a counterplot against Emperor Arian's chamberlain.

# Chapter Ten

"A thousand pardons for my clumsiness, Chamberlain," Pier Norlin said insincerely. He sneered at Tidzio as he backed away. He swiftly hid the small vapor injector he had used on the chamberlain's upper arm. The movement wasn't quick enough to keep it from the wizened man's suspicious eyes.

Tidzio moved to grab Norlin's arm, but Trahnee intervened.

"When is the audience with the emperor, Tidzio?" she asked. "We do not want to be late. Let us go and wait outside his audience chamber, since we do not wish to anger Emperor Arian. Let us do so, and you have nothing to fear."

She worked to move him along on the course already plotted and away from fear about the injection. Tidzio rubbed his upper arm and glared at Norlin, unsure what to do. A snap of his fingers would bring down laser fire from a dozen bodyguards.

He did not act. The emperor demanded Norlin's presence. Arian thwarted was a deadly adversary.

The ten-meter-tall single-crystal diamond doors began opening. Norlin and Trahnee quickly pushed to the front of the small crowd waiting to be granted Emperor Arian's benediction for the day.

"He knows I did something, but he can't decide how dangerous it is," Norlin said. He passed the injector to Trahnee, who immediately gave it to Oloroun as the alien bounced by. If Tidzio demanded a search, they would be innocents set upon by a paranoid chamberlain.

Tidzio did not demand the search. Norlin held his surge of triumph that his scheme was working in check. They were far from getting away from Earth with their lives.

The order to arrest Liottey and Barse had been issued but not executed yet; Tidzio's personal police held them in their quarters aboard the *Preceptor* at Star's End. A little more pressure on the chamberlain would remove even this threat to his crew. He played a dangerous game with a master conspirator, but he had no other choice.

Bells rang and lights flashed. Emperor Arian demanded their presence. He and Trahnee slowly advanced on the sonorous, chirping wood floor, eyes downcast. Norlin couldn't help wondering what other feet had scuffed this floor so smooth over the centuries.

The first of the great galactic emperors had been less inclined to stand on formality and more interested in results. Cameron the Magnificent had forged an empire spanning fourteen colony worlds in addition to Earth and the two nearby settled systems of Alpha Centauri and Epsilon Eridani. The centuries had not fulfilled the promise given the empire by this first and, to Norlin's mind, greatest emperor. Too many of his successors had been venal, mad or, worse, both mad *and* venal, like Arian.

Still, Pier Norlin was an officer in the Empire Service and his allegiance went to those who led it. Only through civil order could there be peace—or a successfully waged war against the invading alien death fleet.

They stopped at the foot of the Crystal Throne.

"My darling Captain Norlin," rumbled the emperor's voice from above. Norlin thought he amplified it to get the impressive bass vibrato. "You are more brilliant than I thought. Why did you hide your ingenuity from me for so long?"

"Nothing can be hidden long from a man such as yourself, Majesty," Norlin replied, not sure what the madman referred to.

"Your plan to invade this Black Nebula displays resourcefulness. I commend you for it. I have spoken with my strategists, and they agree that, for one who is not genhanced, it is clever, indeed."

"Thank you, Majesty," Norlin said, trying to keep the sarcasm from his voice.

He and Trahnee stared at the ruler now they had been spoken to. Arian sat crossed-legged on the Crystal Throne, toys of all varieties scattered around his elevated seat.

"We need a good war. These Kindarians are intruding, destroying *my* colonies. That cannot be permitted. No, not at all. My officers agree with me on this point. And you have done a great service to the empire by bringing this matter to my attention."

Arian chuckled and played with his toys for a minute before speaking again. Norlin and Trahnee simply waited. There was nothing else they could do.

"A war. That is a splendid idea, and we shall do it."

"Majesty, the Kindarian Death Fleet threatens Alpha Centauri."

"Who cares? It's nothing but a big space station, too big to support easily."

"It represents much to the people of Earth—and the empire. AlphaCent was the first system reached by our forefathers."

The emperor clucked patronizingly.

"It was reached by non-genhanced pioneers. That doesn't matter. It was simple to do. Only what transpired after we genhanced took charge matters. That's when real history begins."

"You are authorizing the Empire Service fleet to invade the Black Nebula?" asked Norlin, not sure what the ruler meant by "waging a war." Lying in wait and destroying a major segment of the Death Fleet at Alpha Centauri would reduce the enemy's strength significantly—and preserve the integrity and safety of other colony worlds.

It also protected Earth.

"The ES fleet is in need of a new leader, a war chief such as those the ancient AmerInds used for important fighting," said Emperor Arian. "I am promoting you, Captain. You are now admiral. You will form the fleet, you will drill them unmercifully—do it where I may see the results of your brutal exercises—and then lead them to victory in this Black Nebula."

Norlin stared at Emperor Arian in disbelief.

"You have chosen well, Majesty," said Trahnee, filling in the silence. "Admiral Norlin will serve the empire and you well."

"Of course he will. My strategists all tell me he will, even if he isn't genhanced."

"He is a good choice," Trahnee said, her voice vibrant with the subsonics that convinced and invigorated.

"I know he is," the emperor said petulantly. "All my advisers told me he was a good choice, the ones that survived, that is."

From the tremor in his voice, Arian had succumbed to Trahnee's suggestions, repeating what she wanted him to believe.

"I am pleased that even Chamberlain Tidzio approved," Norlin said.

"Tidzio isn't one of my advisers. Not on Empire Service business. He runs things around the palace and nowhere else. He ought to be working on a banquet to celebrate your promotion. It will make the one last night seem tame in comparison!"

"Majesty, I must return to Star's End and begin work. The fleet needs to be drilled," he said. "Further, my officers require immediate briefing on what might bring the most glory to the greatest emperor on the Crystal Throne since Cameron forged the empire."

"Of course, do it, do it," Emperor Arian said, already distracted and considering other topics.

"You have not made a mistake, Majesty," said Trahnee.

"No, I have not made a mistake. It isn't possible that I can make a mistake. Now, leave, go, go!"

They backed away.

✳ ✳ ✳

Oloroun stood beside the diamond gates, a smirk on his furry face. Indicating that he had disposed of the vapor injector, the Prothasian dashed away, cutting capers like an ancient court jester. Norlin hoped that Arian saw more in the small alien than a furry, funny being, but he doubted it. Ever the arrogant genenhanced, Tidzio had underestimated his intelligence and determination.

"Admiral Norlin," the chamberlain called as they stepped outside the throne room. "May I have a word?"

"How may I serve you?" Norlin tried not to smile too broadly. He knew the game he played—and how easily he and his crew might yet be killed on a whim of the emperor if the effect of Trahnee's verbal spell waned. The man who held the emperor's ear stood before him, hunched over and looking as if he would slay without hesitation.

"The fluid you so clumsily injected into me. What was it?"

"Injection?" Norlin said. "I can't tell you that. It was prepared by others."

"A poison? Was that it? A slow-acting poison? I've had tests run by my personal physicians, and they find nothing."

"Slow-acting viruses from the colony worlds—which ones I am not at liberty to say—often take years to gestate and kill," said Norlin. "But it would be ridiculous to think I carried such dangerous viral agents with me. Or that I know how to defeat such infections. I am only a military officer, not a doctor versed in arcane viruses."

"What do you want?"

"Trahnee," Norlin asked, "where is that order we wanted our dear friend and true ally to examine?"

The genhanced woman silently handed a sheet of paper to Tidzio. The chamberlain seized it and scanned the length quickly. His face clouded with dark anger. Norlin thought their problems might end here with a sudden stroke taking the diminutive man's life. His hands shook until the ripples passed up the embroidered sleeves of his expensive court robe and turned his entire body into an quaking pillar.

"This is an outrage!"

"Why?" Trahnee asked mildly. "Admiral Norlin needs his engineer and first officer to fulfill the mission given him by Emperor Arian. You aren't thinking of countermanding an order given by His Majesty, are you?"

"If I cancel their arrest order, what will you do?"

"I can do nothing, since I am unaware of what your predicament is," said Norlin. "However," he went on smoothly when he saw the rage flushing Tidzio's face, "I might be able to suggest a regimen that can rid the body of unwanted…poisons."

Tidzio swung around angrily and touched a computer keypad mounted on the wall. He spent several seconds entering his access code then finished off the string of numbers that revoked his earlier order.

"It's done. My police on Star's End have been withdrawn."

"We'll check with my crew," said Norlin. "Then we'll be in touch. Don't stray far."

"And do not, under any circumstances, go out in the direct sunlight," Trahnee added maliciously.

Tidzio paled.

Norlin and Trahnee hurried off to get a shuttle to the space station. Norlin said softly, "It's amazing how effective a simple injection of sterile water can have on a man with a suspicious mind."

"We've got to get into space before he figures it out," said Trahnee.

"He won't. Only Oloroun knows of our little deception."

Norlin picked up the pace, however, and almost ran toward their quarters. He had already packed and wanted to be at the royal shuttle before Tidzio worked out another way to attack them.

## ✳ ✳ ✳

"A damned admiral," grumbled Tia Barse. "I don't believe it. And the *Preceptor*'s the flagship?"

"Those are Emperor Arian's wishes," Norlin said, settling into the cruiser's command chair. He put on the heads-up display helmet and powered it up to full detail.

A dazzling readouts array flashed in front of his eyes. Using chin switches and the controls on the arms of his chair, he worked through the command systems and subsystems until he was certain everything had been repaired and they were at full power.

"Captain," said Chikako Miza, "I'm patched through to your ten squadron commanders. You want to talk to them?"

Norlin glanced at the displays and knew Star's End would be too dangerous for him in a little while. Chamberlain Tidzio did not take threats to his power lightly. When he decided to risk the imaginary virus in his bloodstream, the order for their destruction would be issued. Norlin wanted to seize the reins of power before that happened.

"Right away."

He cleared his throat and glanced at Trahnee, who stood a pace away. Her presence helped calm him. A man his age ought to be a sub-commander and nothing higher. He now commanded the Empire Service fleet on a major mission for the emperor.

"Brevet Fleet Admiral Norlin," he announced, "to all fleet communications officers. A com blackout is now in effect." He checked to be sure he had the proper sequence. "Code red, code blue, code three-three."

Throughout the ten squadrons—*his* ten squadrons—communications officers switched to the frequency designated by his orders.

Chikako Miza sent out a scrambled microburst on that frequency and tied all the ships together with a new set of codes and shifting com frequencies. Lasers flashed and established that Norlin was permitted to do this; then, the fleet was cut off from further contact, either to or from Earth.

"On whose authority are you blacking us out?" demanded one battleship captain. "We always stay in contact with the emperor when in the system."

"These are special maneuvers," Norlin answered. "Emperor Arian is keyed through the *Preceptor*."

"Let me talk with him."

"Those are not my orders. You do not question my rank. You will *not* question the emperor's command."

Trahnee whispered to him, "That is Captain Galimeer, a genhanced officer close to the emperor. Some say he is the emperor's favorite, in bed and out."

"All the genhanced think they are," scoffed Norlin.

"In this case, it might be true," Trahnee warned.

"Pass along my orders," Norlin said, coming to a decision. "You can convince him."

"You want me to…"

"*Convince* him," Norlin repeated.

Trahnee's powerfully persuasive genhanced voice could calm a proton storm—or create one. She moved closer to the command chair and spoke quickly to Galimeer while Norlin turned his attention elsewhere.

"Captain," spoke up Sarov. "We're not getting response codes from all the ships. They've refused to key on to our battle computer."

The vidscreen flashed with the holes left by those units not linking with Sarov's board.

"Mitri, prepare to destroy any ship not linked in one minute. Chikako, pass along the order. Barse, get the radiation cannon ready for use. Liottey, see that all systems are ready for combat."

While his officers prepared to enforce his orders to the fleet, he jockeyed the *Preceptor* from dock. The immense cruiser drifted away then used steering jets to maneuver them into a higher orbit. Only then did he cut in the main drive and send them rocketing outward on a trajectory designed to put them within lasartillery firing distance of Galimeer's battleship.

"What's the status?" he asked Trahnee.

She shook her head.

"Galimeer is too confident. He is positive he can go over your head to the emperor. I heard him order his communications officer to ready a laser link directly with the emperor's palace. If he doesn't get through to Arian, I am sure he can contact Tidzio."

"Chikako, scramble that com-link to Earth from the battleship *Stormer*."

"No good, Captain," reported his com officer. "They're already linked. I can't tap it or snap it."

"Captain Galimeer," Norlin said, "you are in direct violation of my orders. Surrender your command immediately to your first officer. This is an act of mutiny and will not be tolerated."

"Norlin, I am confirming your orders. The emperor will give me mine. You aren't even genhanced."

"Sarov, burn out the *Stormer*'s laser com nodule."

"Firing now," came the tactical officer's gruff acknowledgement.

Pandemonium reigned as the *Preceptor* blew off the battleship's primary communication unit.

"Prepare for all-out battle," Norlin said over his private circuits to his officers. "Use the radiation cannon. There's no other way to take out a battleship."

"Captain, I might be able to do it if their tac officer's not on the job," said Sarov. "A timed array of missiles might sneak up their rocket tubes."

"Try that first. Keep the radiation cannon at ready if you can't disable the ship," he ordered.

His hands turned clammy. The overworked conditioning elements inside his heads-up display failed to keep the sweat from pouring down into his eyes. Data from all over the ship came to him. He absorbed it and took appropriate action. Faster and faster it came. The computers did their job, but he had to make the decisions.

He was the *Preceptor*'s captain; he had to establish himself as the Empire Service fleet's admiral.

"You blew off my laser com, you peasant son of a bitch!" roared Galimeer. "You can't do this."

"Attention, all ships in the Empire Service fleet, the *Stormer* has mutinied. Appropriate action will be taken."

"Jamming radio frequencies, Captain," said Chikako. "I'm using a combination of my own technique and one I picked up from the Kindarians. There's not much getting through that mush. Lasercom is being disrupted, too."

The hiss and crackle almost deafened him—and Chikako had filtered out most of it so that he could maintain contact while the other ships were isolated.

The approach computer and Sarov warned him simultaneously that the *Stormer* was prepared for battle.

"Take him out, Sarov. Do it now," ordered Norlin.

He took no joy in seeing missiles launched against another ship in the Empire Service—that battleship might mean the difference between victory and defeat when they went to cut the heart out of the Kindarian homeworld. He also knew that if discipline and authority were not established now, there would be no invasion of the Black Nebula.

Norlin wasn't even sure the emperor meant him to be in command. Emperor Arian had odd ideas of training maneuvers and "fun."

"Interdicting response missiles," said Sarov. "They're not doing a very good job of it. Their computer is using a basic attack pattern. Simple to stop."

Battle had honed their tactics, and this cruel experience was used with success in the attack against the *Stormer*. Norlin watched as Sarov's volley homed in on the tail section of Galimeer's ship.

One missile snaked through the defending lasartillery fire and exploded, ripping away a large chunk of engine.

"He's not going anywhere with that damage, Captain," said Sarov.

"Galimeer's trying to reach Chamberlain Tidzio. Still blocking the signal. Good thing we learned so much about signal blocking from the Kindarians."

"What of the other ships, Pier?" asked Trahnee. "What of them?"

"They're standing clear. If we bring Galimeer to heel, they'll follow. If not, they'll tear us to bloody shreds."

"They refuse to surrender," said Sarov. "The *Stormer*'s inertial platforms are swinging about. Lasartillery is trained on us. New volleys of missiles are on the way—they outnumber us five to one on launch tubes."

Even as Sarov spoke, the *Preceptor* accelerated wildly to avoid the rain of genius missiles launched by the heavier, better-armed and -armored battleship. The *Stormer* might be unable to use its engines, but it remained a formidable opponent.

"Can we take the ship, Sarov?"

"Too much power against us, Captain. They're determined to go down fighting."

And Norlin was determined to take them down fast.

"Barse, is the switch ready for the radiation cannon?"

"Ready, Cap'n," the engineer reported.

Pier Norlin took a deep breath then set the firing computer. A single light blinked on his control panel. The captured Kindarian radiation cannon took the lives of scores more humans aboard the *Stormer*.

# Chapter Eleven

N othing?" roared Chamberlain Tidzio. "There is *nothing* in my bloodstream?"

"No exotic poison, no unusual virus, no strange infective agent imported from the colony worlds," confirmed the doctor.

"I'll cut off your ears and force you to eat them if you're wrong."

The threat did not faze the doctor. Tidzio started to magnify the threat then realized he would be unable to carry through should there be some insidious agent creeping through his body. He prided himself on being aware of every death-dealing agent possible. He also realized the doctor might be right, and that the accursed barbarian had played mind games. Tidzio would not have credited a colonist with such finesse. It had to be the genhanced bitch's plan. Only another genhanced could perpetrate such treachery.

"You are unchanged from this time yesterday," the doctor said, giving his readouts a final glance.

"Out. Get out. I won't let that young jackanapes do this to me. I, the most powerful man in the Empire!"

Tidzio fumed and stalked around his quarters. He had been duped into releasing the hold he had over Pier Norlin.

The colonial officer was a fool. He permitted feelings to get in his way. Tidzio had seen this immediately and had worked to use it against him. The reversal of the scheme to bind Norlin permanently infuriated him. Norlin had left Earth, and Tidzio held no sway over him. If the new admiral maintained communications blackout for his one-hundred-ship fleet, Tidzio might never regain control. That fleet constituted too large a threat to allow. He had to neutralize Norlin's influence quickly.

The initial rage faded, and Tidzio's sharp mind spun through the details of the turnabout. Norlin had not been in the emperor's court long enough to learn the details of the plan forming against him. Trahnee might have the contacts—she had been banished once because of her damnable genhanced talents. Tidzio had watched them carefully until the night when so many of his schemes had required his personal attention. His memories cast back, and he remembered every detail perfectly. Who had he seen? How had they responded? Did he remember anything out of the ordinary happening?

He could not decide the agent of his misfortune. Norlin and Trahnee had allied themselves with a power faction at court. Who? Who had thwarted him so effectively?

Tidzio vented his rage and shrieked loudly.

✳ ✳ ✳

Through the spyhole in the wall, Oloroun watched and thrilled to the sight of the impotent chamberlain. Tidzio had never considered him a threat. He mistakenly thought Oloroun was but a moment's diversion for the emperor. Cavorting and rolling and pretending to speak poorly amused everyone—and robbed the humans of their normal suspicions.

He continued to watch as Tidzio formulated new plans against Norlin.

The chamberlain began by fabricating evidence of treason against the emperor. Clever computer work produced the documents, the events, substantiating witnesses—everything needed to prove a strong case of disloyalty to the empire. By the time he was finished, Tidzio had made Norlin out to be the worst traitor since Woodlan had sold out to rebels for a mere handful of gold coins.

Oloroun studied the computer screen, memorized the details then dashed off along his secret passage. He had work of his own to do to counter the chamberlain's expertise at lying.

✳ ✳ ✳

The radiation cannon left the *Stormer* a lifeless hulk. Norlin sagged and shook his head. Galimeer had thought to seize control of the fleet and had underestimated the lengths Norlin would go to defend his newfound position.

Hw couldn't allow even one genhanced officer to think he was superior. To do so would reduce the fleet to squabbling units, each run like an ancient feudal fiefdom. Ten captains each commanded ten ships. Those hundred, with the *Preceptor*, formed the fleet that had to strike into the heart of Kindarian territory and destroy another empire. Even the loss of one battleship affected his plans.

"There will be no further rebellion," he said quietly into the intership com-link Chikako Miza had established. The frequencies changed thousands of times a second according to the pattern established by his initial code sequence. No one on Earth could intercept these communications and orders.

He hoped the com officers maintained their silence and didn't try to contact Earth—Arian or Tidzio—directly. His orders would be overridden in a flash.

The announcement that he had destroyed the *Stormer* caused the channel to buzz with complaints.

"Trahnee," he said, "talk to them. Tell them they are officers in the Empire Service, and they obey their superiors. Tell them I'm their superior."

"You want me to influence them," she said.

Norlin nodded tiredly. He didn't want to use her talents in this fashion, but he had no real choice. To lose the fleet now imperiled not only the colonies but Earth itself. While they remained near Earth within Tidzio's reach, he might lose his only chance to save humanity.

Of Chikako he asked, "Any sign of Death Fleet intrusion into the solar system?"

"There are hints," she said. "I need to study the sensors seeded beyond Pluto's orbit to be sure. The station on Charon might record what we need. I don't know."

"It will not," cut in Sarov. "I studied the fire-control facilities available from there. It is hardly more than a punishment post. No real defense can be mounted from there."

This suited Norlin. From everything he had read, Pluto's larger satellite was a dreary, cold lump of rock, not unlike its primary. Best to rely on their own observations.

He worked through the data they had accumulated in the Alpha Centauri system. He saw the pattern forming as the computer worked to analyze the constant flow of information. The alien death fleet would burn through Alpha Centauri and race directly to Earth. The Kindarians would think AlphaCent was a warning post, a first line of defense that needed to be destroyed before the real invasion, of the human homeworld, could begin.

"They'll give us some warning," Norlin said. "Keep monitoring conditions at Alpha Centauri."

"Cap'n, why not just take the fleet there and wait for the Kindarians?"

Norlin wrestled with the suggested change in strategy. He had orders, but how did they limit him?

"Tia, you've got a good idea. There's nothing in my orders requiring me to drill the fleet inside the solar system."

"We can use a shakedown battle or two," Barse went on. "Half of those space-sucking worms will be killed off. They aren't fighters. They spend most of their time toadying up to the emperor."

"And his chamberlain," said Norlin. He had seen how unrestricted Tidzio was. Emperor Arian was seldom able to put more than a few minutes of coherent thought into any project; he ruled by whim and emotion. Tidzio did the long-range planning for the realm and wielded the true power.

Trahnee clicked off and said to him, "The nine surviving subfleet commanders will follow you. I have convinced them that the *Preceptor*'s armament is superior to theirs—and that they stand a better chance for promotion backing you than going over your head to Tidzio or the emperor."

"So much for my innate leadership qualities and other sterling talents," he said sarcastically. Trahnee smiled at him.

"You should be happy they'll follow with so little persuasion. Take command of the nine ships left by Captain Galimeer.

Use them as a cadre to enforce discipline in the other units. Gali-meer, for all his faults, was a skilled commander. He's left you with nine of the best."

Norlin flipped on the vidscreen and scanned the nine ships. A midget battleship, three Nova class cruisers and five destroy-ers comprised the sub-fleet. Norlin contacted each ship's cap-tain in turn and formed them behind him in a conical array, the *Preceptor* at the vertex and the base of the cone almost two light-minutes distant.

"You're precious to me, Trahnee," he said softly. "For many reasons." He reached out and touched her cheek.

She took his hand, kissed it and said, "I have to go back to Earth. That's the only way I can overthrow the emperor."

"I need you here. We can deal with Emperor Arian and Tidzio when we—"

"Pier, I have to go *now*. You've seen how conditions are. They are even worse now than when Bo and I were a part of the court. Tidzio lets Arian rage unchecked. The empire cannot survive such virulence and decay at its head."

"The colonies will break away eventually," Norlin said. "The alliance holding them to Earth has become more tenuous over the years. Now that the Death Fleet has destroyed several and the others are asking what the emperor did to stop it…" He let the words trail off. The empire existed only through historical inertia. A fresh wind would blow across the worlds and send them on their own course, independent of Earth's.

Soon.

"The Death Fleet might get past us. Space is the safest place you can be," he said.

"I've never sought safety, Pier. You, of all people, know that. Return me to Earth. When you finish in the Black Nebula, you'll find the empire transformed. I may not be on the Crystal Throne, but someone will who can rule sensibly."

"A genhanced?"

"We make the best rulers," she said simply.

He shook his head. "I've seen no evidence of that. For each flash of genius, there are days of depravity and madness. I don't know how you escaped that insanity."

"I don't have to be a mind reader to know you're wondering if I *do* escape what you think is normal for one of the genhanced. Emperor Arian and Tidzio are not the norm."

Norlin doubted her contention. He had seen genhanced officers along the frontier, and they were all brilliant and flirted with insanity

"You have to go, don't you?"

"Not right away." Her poignant expression carried more command, for him, than her genhanced voice ever could. Duty tore at her just as it did him.

"Lieutenant-Commander Sarov, you have the conn," he said, slipping from the command chair. Sarov grunted and mumbled about taking time away from his battle simulation studies. Norlin didn't bother looking back. He and Trahnee had too little time together before she shuttled to Earth and he took the Empire Service fleet to Alpha Centauri to engage the Kindarians.

\* \* \*

Trahnee stretched, trying to work the stiffness from her arms and legs. The small descent capsule Tia Barse had put her in gave little opportunity for movement. The trip through Earth's atmosphere had been quick and hot, most of the capsule shell ablating. Trahnee stared at the exterior of the eggshell she had ridden to ground from space and marveled that it had endured such fierce heat.

She shivered. Another few hundred meters of burning descent and she might have vaporized. A single hole through the thin hull would have meant her death.

She looked around and got her bearings. If she stayed here too long, her death might be assured from other quarters. Tidzio had an efficient spy network throughout the Empire Service. A controller must have witnessed her fiery descent and reported it through channels—and directly to the chamberlain, because it was an extraordinary event.

Finding the underground opposition to the emperor that she knew existed might be difficult. For her, though, it wasn't impossible. She regretted having to leave Pier Norlin, but his mission wasn't hers. The threat posed by the Kindarians was great, but to her mind that posed by Tidzio and the genhanced emperor was greater.

She walked from the ruined descent capsule and found a levitrain station less than two kilometers away. The blunt-nosed superconducting bullet flashed by the platform. She tried to figure out when the train might stop at this station and couldn't because the posted schedule had been so defaced. This might be nothing more than a cargo dock—or an emergency station for troop movement. Emperor Arian had increasing problems with rioting, she had learned during her brief stay at the palace. Some stations might be dedicated only to moving riot police across the face of the planet.

"Eagle," she said aloud. A slow smile crossed her face.

She knew Eagle. He had been a minor leader of a rebel faction when she and Bo had been exiled. Contacting him would be easy enough.

Trahnee found the control center for the levitrain station and broke into the main office. Of human controllers she found no trace. The few robotic ones offered no opposition to her as she called Eagle.

He did not greet her wholeheartedly but did agree to meet her. She could ask for nothing more than that. For the moment.

✳ ✳ ✳

"Oloroun is our friend," she told Simon Grendel, code name Eagle. Grendel stared at the small alien and shook his head sadly.

"You have been among the colonists too long, Trahnee. *This* is our way of striking out against the emperor? We need to foment revolt among the *genhanced* if we are to hope to succeed."

"*This*, as you call him, is a very intelligent being. The Prothasians were conquered, but that doesn't mean they are stupid or nothing more than cuddly little pets. That's what makes Oloroun so valuable to us. No one in the palace takes him seriously."

"Nor do I," said Grendel. He rose to his full two-meter height and scowled so hard his dark eyes almost disappeared. As if wanting to vanish from sight, he drew his coarse brown cloak about his thin shoulders, finally saying, "I had hoped we could work together. I see I was wrong. You entertain foolish hopes of overthrowing Arian using a…bear."

"They're not foolish with Oloroun acting as our inside contact," Trahnee insisted. Her voice hummed with convincing subsonics.

Grendel shook his head, as if trying to clear a buzzing from his ears. He stared at her and tried to speak. His mouth opened and closed, no words coming forth.

"We can do it. You have the personnel, I have the contact," said Trahnee.

She glanced at Oloroun. He was hunkered down in one corner of the room in the otherwise deserted levitrain station, uneasy at being away from the palace. She had asked him about his travels across Earth and had found that Tidzio kept him always inside, either through design or malice. The thought of sneaking out to this meeting had filled the Prothasian with an apprehension approaching phobia.

"Tidzio must be stopped," Oloroun said. "The emperor is nothing without him."

"Don't be duped into thinking that," Trahnee said. "Arian is not the fool he seems. Endanger him, and he drops the façade of drooling idiot."

"We must kill Emperor Arian *and* Tidzio," said Grendel. "The bloodbath can be restricted to only a few hundred if we chop off their heads. Otherwise, we might have to kill hundreds of thousands in the Empire Service."

"The military will follow us if the emperor and chamberlain are gone," said Trahnee. She and Bo had spent long hours working on these plans and had decided the military had no loyalty to the emperor; their loyalties lay with power and those wielding it. Most senior officers were genhanced and, therefore amenable to logical argument concerning allegiance. Nothing appealed more to the officer corps than winning and being led by winners.

"Oloroun gets us into the palace," she continued, "and your squad does the rest."

"Getting inside the palace is impossible," Grendel protested. "We've tried. Each time we've done nothing but lose valuable personnel. Tidzio is a frightened little dwarf. He guards the palace jealously and well."

"I can get us in," said Oloroun. "I got out, didn't I?"

"We need him, Grendel. Be the eagle you use for a code name. Soar!"

Trahnee's enthusiasm was contagious. She added more than a little of her genhanced persuasion to it. Grendel agreed, reluctantly at first and then with more enthusiasm until he was certain this had been his own idea.

"How long will it take to get a squad of assassins ready?" Trahnee asked. "Oloroun can get us in any time we want. It ought to be soon."

Grendel touched a com-link on his lapel. Trahnee spun and saw a dozen men and women armed with laser rifles appear out of thin air. They had been hiding, and she had not caught any sign of them before this instant.

"They're good," said Grendel. "Let's see if your furry friend is as good as he claims. Let's go to the palace now and do some killing."

"A moment," said Oloroun. "I have a demand to make."

"What?" Grendel and Trahnee chorused. The genhanced woman motioned Grendel to silence then asked the Prothasian, "What is your condition for helping us?"

"It is not much, not much," said Oloroun. "I want to kill Tidzio. He has humiliated me for the last time, the last time, yes, the very last time!"

Trahnee didn't know whether to laugh or be frightened. With the same genhanced arrogance that besotted Tidzio and Arian, she had assumed superiority in all things. Their plots and counterplots meant they ignored everyone else around them at the emperor's court as inferiors. She had misjudged the small alien completely. Such wrong judgments boded ill for their future.

# Chapter Twelve

"All elements, prepare to shift to Alpha Centauri," Pier Norlin ordered. It bothered him that he was the commander for the Empire Service fleet and had not gone through any significant drills with units that might—or might not—obey him. Compared to the hundreds—thousands!—of ships in the Kindarian Death Fleet, this was a small unit. For the empire, it represented more than half the entire ES space force defending Earth.

Yet he *was* the admiral in charge. The burdens of command weighed heavily on him, especially now that Trahnee had returned to Earth. Even if he didn't use her genhanced talent to whip the other commanders into order, having her beside him had provided support he got in no other way.

"Ready, Admiral," came the reply from the nine sub-commanders under his direct orders. He glanced at Sarov's and Chikako Miza's readouts and saw that everything was in readiness.

"We shift on my command and come out ready for action," he continued.

During the short four-light-year shift, they would be out of contact with all other vessels. When they dropped back into normal space, they might find the Kindarian fleet already at work destroying the AlphaCent space station and turning their deadly beams on terraforming facilities planetside. Regrouping then to attack might prove too difficult if they were more occupied with simply surviving.

Better to go into the shift in good order than to die trying to maneuver into battle formation at the other side of shift space.

"What of our prisoner?" he asked Liottey, switching on the vidcam in the cell and staring at the Kindarian. The alien remained hunched over, four spindly legs tucked under him.

"Can't tell his condition, Captain," replied the first officer. "He's uncommunicative and dangerous to get near. As ordered, I had him sealed in a compartment while the ship was in dry dock so none of the emperor's staff would see him. He spits whenever I try to feed him."

"You've let the robots do the actual tending, haven't you?" asked Norlin. He didn't want to lose Liottey now that he was proving himself a worthy officer. The alien's digestive juices were potent, indeed, to burn through a composite wall. What that might do to human flesh wasn't anything Norlin wanted to explore.

"Yes, sir. I've also revamped the life support system. Sarov and I ran the equations through his battle computer to maximize use of equipment and minimize repair times."

"Your report is noted," Norlin said, seeing it in his to-be-read queue. When he had time he would study it. Now, he simply trusted that Liottey had done the work properly and that Sarov would have reported any major problem with the first officer's reprogramming of their robot repair units.

"Barse," he called out, getting his engineer on a private circuit, "is everything ready? When we get back to normal space, we'll be fighting."

"We can fight now, Cap'n," she said. "It's good to be back in action. I didn't enjoy sitting around Star's End with my finger up my butt."

"Strap the cat down when we shift back. There's no way to predict, but I believe we'll be in the middle of a battle within seconds."

"Neutron will lend a paw. I've got him strapped over a port, and we can use him for an extra steering jet if we have to. Or we can ignite his methane and burn the hell out of those spiders if the weaponry goes down."

Norlin chuckled as he switched off. Barse had a way about her he liked. His entire crew did. They were mismatched but had come to work as a team. That, more than anything else, endeared them to him.

His thoughts turned back to Trahnee and her mission on Earth. He hoped she would be successful. Norlin clenched his fists and knew that success might be as elusive for her as it would be for the *Preceptor*.

✳ ✳ ✳

Grendel motioned for his squad to fan out as they crossed the neatly groomed palace grounds. In spite of Oloroun's assurance that Tidzio did not maintain surveillance on this portion of the palace, the rebel exercised extreme caution approaching the southern wing.

"Here," said the Prothasian. "This is my den. You are welcome here. No one snoops." Oloroun had run down the corridors and skidded to a halt in front of his sleeping chambers.

One by one, Grendel's squad drifted into the room until it was crowded. Trahnee sat beside Oloroun. Grendel faced them, shifting around on his knees for comfort. Even so, his head brushed the low ceiling.

"We've got this far, which is better than we've been able to do in the past. If I remember the layout, we're less than five hundred meters from Arian's sleeping chambers."

"When he's on the Crystal Throne is a better time to take him," Trahnee decided. "There is a certain justice to attacking then."

Grendel nodded. He, too, liked the idea of killing the emperor on the Crystal Throne.

"What of Tidzio?" he asked.

"He is in chambers not far from here," said Oloroun. "Straying is not in his nature. He stays close. Very, very close. Guards walk everywhere, and he uses gnat-sized cameras to spy."

"You weren't joking when you said he would come in handy," Grendel said to Trahnee. "Where are the guards? I don't care about the vidcams. We'll be seen sooner or later. The trick is to strike fast and be sure of our targets."

"Guards on other side of sleeping chambers," Oloroun said, glancing at a small clock hidden in the fake rock walls of his den. "We can walk in now."

"It's too easy," another rebel protested. "There's a trap. A trick. How do we know he is being honest?"

"I want to kill him. I do," declared Oloroun. "To pass up this chance is not my way."

"We've come too far to back out now. Let's do it," declared Grendel. "It makes me nervous just sitting around. Everyone knows their role. We've practiced enough times."

Trahnee hesitated once Grendel and his squad wiggled free of Oloroun's den and stood in the corridor. She wanted to accompany them but didn't want to be in the way.

"With me," urged Oloroun. "Come with me. You are my friend. I want you to witness Tidzio's death at my hand." His paw flashed deadly claws as he raked the air.

She nodded and silently padded after him.

Grendel split his forces, half going to the throne room in the hope of finding the emperor there. The rest accompanied Oloroun to the chamberlain's quarters. Trahnee had to admit to a bias. Killing Tidzio seemed more important to her than deposing Arian.

She paused outside Tidzio's door. Grendel and three others readied their laserifles. They would burst in firing.

"Mine," Oloroun reminded them. "He is mine. Let me in first. Follow in seconds."

"You promised," Trahnee said, using just a hint of her persuasive powers to convince Grendel.

The rebel leader nodded and motioned for the Prothasian to precede them.

Oloroun quietly opened the door, then moved in a blur of speed. Grendel didn't wait. He followed immediately, laserifle leveled and ready.

"Not here!" cried Oloroun. "Chamberlain is elsewhere!"

"The alarms!" cried Trahnee, pointing.

The small computer Tidzio used to plot his nefarious schemes flared with red lights and warning signals. She rushed to it and magnified the vidscreen display for the others to see.

"The emperor's guards stopped the others," she said. "All six of them are dead. And there's no trace of Tidzio." She looked at Oloroun and Grendel. "We've got to get out of here."

Grendel was already at the door, his weapon moving restlessly, ready to kill anyone waiting for them outside.

"The way's clear," he said in disbelief.

Oloroun and Trahnee joined him and the others in headlong retreat from the palace.

They returned to the levitrain depot. Of those who had tried to assassinate the emperor they saw no trace. Breathless, Trahnee was glad to have escaped with her life so easily. Too easily?

There would be other days, other battles—she hoped. Arian was always paranoid but now might find an intellectual challenge in a new rebel offensive to amuse him. Reaching him now would be infinitely more difficult.

✳ ✳ ✳

"All hands, prepare to exit shift space," Norlin said. He settled his command helmet on his head and adjusted the displays to give him only the highlights from each of the *Preceptor*'s major systems. Weapons, drive and power, vector and approach—all fed into his heads-up display.

He rested the samurai sword Emperor Arian had given him across his lap, his fingers dancing over the intricate engraving on the sheath. He knew what those ancient warriors had felt before they entered battle—this feeling of excitement he shared completely.

"Dropping out of shift space…now!" cried Barse.

The ship entered normal space in the Alpha Centauri system—and found themselves less than twenty light-seconds from the advance elements of the Kindarian Death Fleet.

"I knew it!" Norlin cried, feeling vindicated. The timing had been right for the Kindarians to enter the system and attack. How long they had been hammering away at the huge space station circling the barren world he didn't know.

And it didn't matter. He triggered the *Preceptor*'s lasartillery immediately and took out an unsuspecting Kindarian scout ship.

"Regaining contact with other units," Chikako said. "All have successfully shifted free."

"Sarov, get them into position. Get them firing at the enemy."

"Too late for three of them," the tac officer said. "The Kindarians got lucky and had radiation cannon pointed directly at a battleship and two destroyers. Am signaling the others to form into standard attack configuration."

Norlin tapped orders into the arm of his chair. The *Preceptor*'s computer translated his wishes into orders for the other sub-fleets. His own unit, all nine of them, had come through the brief shift from Earth in the conical formation. Missiles erupted from their launch tubes and created a curtain of death between the Kindarian heavy battleships and the Alpha Centauri space station.

Norlin worked to implement his ideas, his fingers flying over the computer keys. One by one, he lost contact with other units in his small fleet. The Death Fleet outnumbered his five-to-one, but surprise played an important role in the fight. The Kindarians were targeting the space station; the Empire Service fleet attacked from the rear and racked up an impressive number of early kills.

"Sarov, switch to lasartillery. We're getting too close for the missiles to work without endangering our own forces. It's too confusing in this jungle."

Everywhere he looked on the vidscreen display flashed ships. Even magnifying the scale did little to keep the green dots of his fleet from overlapping the red of the aliens.

"I'm dropping genius missiles that can find an enemy signature and stay with it. The others haven't adjusted their missiles for the Kindarian configuration yet. They aren't going to be as effective." Sarov continued to run computer studies of the battle's progress even as he implemented new defensive and offensive measures. As the results passed across his board, he relayed them to Norlin and the other sub-fleet commanders.

"Let's clean up this mess," Norlin said, seeing an opening in the vidscreen display. He ran a computer check, which verified what he had guessed. He took his five surviving ships directly through the center of the raging battle.

When he had penetrated into the heart of the Kindarian fleet working against the space station, he reformed the sub-fleet into a globe, their main batteries all pointing outward.

"Good tactic," Sarov congratulated. "We all fire in three, two, one, *now!*" Mitri Sarov had smoothly taken control and coordinated the battle to perfection. All the ships fired lasartillery constantly outward in a sphere of death that took out even the heaviest of the Kindarian Death Fleet.

"Got 'em!" cried Norlin. He settled down and tried to control his pounding heart. The adrenaline pumped fiercely in him. They had met the alien death fleet in space and had soundly defeated it. "Subfleets four and seven, pursue the stragglers. No quarter."

He watched as the sixteen surviving ships in the units he had designated split apart from the main battle and went hunting individual Kindarian ships.

The alien scouts had not taken part in the battle; they now tried to flee. With their deadly radiation cannon, they posed a decided threat. Norlin watched as ship after ship of the Empire Service died.

But the aliens died faster.

"Picking up crosstalk from the enemy command ships," reported Chikako. "They're turning tail and running."

"Mark and track," snapped Norlin. He didn't want a single Kindarian to escape unscathed. If he couldn't destroy them all, he'd mark them so they'd know they had been in a battle.

"They're shifting in the direction of Epsilon Eridani," said Chikako. "I wonder if they're rejoining the main fleet."

"What do you mean?" snapped Norlin.

"This is only a quarter of the fleet size that has attacked the colony worlds. It's as if this was a foray to test the strength of resistance—or maybe they didn't think there would be much resistance from a single space station."

Norlin cursed. He had been too caught up in the heat of battle to notice what Miza had seen right away. He had taken heavy losses and hadn't decisively defeated a major enemy fleet at all.

"How bad a beating did we take?" he asked Liottey. His first officer had done a good job repairing what damage they had sustained in the combat.

"We're one hundred percent. Casualties throughout the fleet total, sixteen ships totally destroyed, nineteen others damaged and incapable of further engagement."

Norlin sighed. He had lost thirty-five percent of his entire fleet against a small element of the Kindarian Death Fleet. In victory, he had lost.

"The aliens," Liottey went on, "lost eighteen battleships, nine heavy cruisers, fourteen destroyer-class ships and more than thirty scout vessels."

"Repeat that," Norlin said, not believing his first officer's numbers.

He punched up the report on his vidscreen display and marveled at it. Alien casualties had been twice the empire fleet's! And the Empire Service fleet had been outnumbered five-to-one.

"Loss of ships and personnel means less to them than being forced to retreat, Captain," said Liottey. "Both on an absolute and percentage basis, we outfought them."

"The space station is reporting. No significant damage. We got to them in time," said Miza.

Norlin began to glow in the warmth of the victory. The fight had been fierce—and the Empire Service had triumphed. His triumph began to fade as he remembered this was only a single battle—perhaps a small one—in a longer war that stretched out to the Black Nebula.

"All unit commanders report immediately," he said over the intership com-link. "We're going after them. All of them!"

The sub-fleet commanders reported. Many of the ships had sustained minor damage but all were in condition to shift.

"We're not letting them enter the Epsilon Eridani system."

"Captain," said Sarov, turning and facing Norlin. "This might be a harder battle for us. Four hundred-plus enemy ships in addition to those that might already be attacking Epsilon Eridani. We might be outnumbered twenty-to-one—or more."

"We're going after them," Norlin said. "We can't leave them this close to Earth. An expedition into the Black Nebula is useless if we return and find the heart of the empire carved out."

He didn't mention his worry over Trahnee's being on Earth. Battling the alien fleet in space kept them away from the planet where his lover was trying to overthrow the emperor.

"Before we shift, let's regroup. We can estimate where the Kindarians are already attacking in the Epsilon Eridani system."

"How badly are we outnumbered?" muttered Sarov. "Sir," he said louder, "we need to emerge from shift space precisely on-target and all batteries firing if we are to stand any chance. AlphaCent will look easy in comparison, since they must know we will follow."

Norlin and Sarov linked with the tac officers on a dozen other ships to work out a new attack pattern. The Death Fleet had left Alpha Centauri. It would be in disarray when it emerged in the Epsilon Eridani system—and Norlin wanted to take advantage of that chaos when they shifted, however long it might exist. The aliens had never been dealt such a defeat. How would they react? Despair? Confusion? Or renewed determination?

Hours later, Norlin and the other commanders had worked out their pre-shift formation.

"It'll be dangerous for an ES ship not precisely locked into the pattern," he said over the intership com-link. "We shift free, then we fire. Missiles on target. Lasartillery. Anything that's alien and in front of you is a target. Lock in the program now." He transmitted the battle orders, then the regrouping and shift commands.

It took another hour before shift. The duration to Epsilon Eridani was seven days, and gave Norlin more than enough time to second-guess his plans and how they might succeed against an alerted Death Fleet.

The *Preceptor* shifted back into normal space in the Epsilon Eridani system and immediately found the enemy.

# Chapter Thirteen

The bridge filled with the stench of burning metal and subli-
mated carbon composite. The *Preceptor* shuddered every time
Norlin demanded power from the engines for a complex, mem-
ber-straining maneuver. Even worse, he was unable to use por-
tions of his internal communications system. He had to shout
instructions over his shoulder to Miza and Sarov.

They had entered the Epsilon Eridani system in the middle of the Kindarian fleet. Norlin had been prepared for it and
had fired instantly, using lasartillery to cut a swath through the
enemy vessels. That had been the last easy victory the *Preceptor*
scored.

The Kindarians fought with a ferocity that stunned Norlin
because he had—naively—expected them to be taken by surprise
and to require time to form effective defenses. He had seen their
viciousness when beaming human settled planets. They gave
no quarter.

They gave none now.

His fleet had entered in formation and had acquitted itself
well until the ship-to-ship com-link had failed. Quantum shot
noise—the static from quantum mechanical fluctuations—disrupted his orders from his computer to those of his nine sub-
commanders. Norlin gave up and simply tried to stay alive.

"We're getting through," called Sarov. "We need the radiation cannon. Use it, Captain."

Norlin triggered the captured alien weapon and blew apart an immense Kindarian battleship designed to eradicate life on planets. Although this momentarily relieved the pressure of battle on them, it also drew the other Death Fleet ships. They recognized the true menace in the ES fleet—the *Preceptor*.

Norlin let his tac officer handle the minute-to-minute fight while he tried to formulate a different strategy. If they did nothing more than go one-on-one with the aliens, they would lose. They were still scoring impressive victories in terms of numbers, but the Kindarians could lose five vessels for every human ship and still win.

"Chikako, patch me through. To hell with the noise. We're driving hard for Epsilon Eridani Two."

"The planet is doing well with its orbiting hardware," the com officer reported. "The weaponry on-planet is taking a good toll of the Kindarians, too."

"We'll press the aliens toward the planet and get support from the planet-based armament. It's the only way we're going to survive. Punch the orders through on laser links."

"That takes a long time, Captain," she protested.

"We've got nothing better to do. Start now. Get the message to the sub-commanders and let them transmit to their vessels."

Norlin winced as he stared at the vidscreen and its graphic display. Two more of his heaviest vessels had been beamed out of existence by the deadly Kindarian cannons. He tried to do a quick count of what he had left in space and failed. The vidscreen was filled with flashing red points for the Death Fleet ships and green for his. Some amber specks appeared—unidentified ships that might belong to either side.

Communications failed across all his boards now; he hoped the laser link messages had gotten through. At the best of times, lasers were difficult to aim, needing alignments too precise for use in the heat of battle. Quantum entanglement com gear had never shown promise, and neutrino communications required too heavy a drain on a ship's power to be useful, especially in battle. The quantum shot noise, coupled with the inherent vacuum noise of photons popping in and out of existence from zero-point energy sources, made it even more difficult to relay his orders. Norlin's only hope was that the other commanders watched and would follow his lead—if they could isolate the *Preceptor* in the flashing morass of ships.

Space was immense, but the two fleets filled this portion of it to overflowing.

Norlin was almost thrown from his command chair

"Missile?" he called out.

"Just debris from another ship," said Chikako. "I wasn't able to track it to give a warning. The section must have been a light-weight composite."

Norlin nodded grimly. A hull section from one of the Empire Service ships. He hoped the debris didn't mean still more death but knew it must.

He toggled the drive engines and rocketed toward Epsilon Eridani II, not caring if they conserved fuel. He had to force the Kindarians closer to the planet and its heavy weapons. For what seemed hours, he watched the vidscreen display. The Death Fleet slowly contracted, consolidating as they dropped toward the planet. This part of his plan had worked. He hoped the rest would, too.

"Got a count on our survivors, Captain," said Sarov. "Eighteen untouched ships, thirty-two damaged but fighting. No contact with the rest. Those are presumed lost."

He checked the *Preceptor*'s systems. None of the major systems had malfunctioned, but everything else had sustained damage amounting to complete destruction. He checked Liottey's station and found the first officer constantly pirating the lesser systems for parts to repair the major. Without his astute repair work, they might have ranked among the destroyed.

"Good work, Gowan," he complimented. He tried to reestablish com to the officers behind him and couldn't. Louder, he called out, "Sarov, systems status. Can we keep firing?"

"Forget the missiles. The tubes are empty. Use the lasartillery or the radiation cannon."

Norlin cursed. He'd wanted to lay down a track of genius missiles behind them as they worked their way toward the planet. If any Kindarian ship tried to escape, the missiles would have immediately tracked and destroyed. He changed his plan again.

They would fight down to the edge of the atmosphere and keep fighting until either the Death Fleet or the Empire Service was destroyed.

The green dots on his vidscreen vanished faster and faster. The red concentrated until he was no longer able to differentiate them. A red band circled Epsilon Eridani II.

"Com back with the other ships?" he asked Chikako.

"We're blind and deaf, Captain."

He made a last check of the ship's support systems, saw that Liottey kept them together and touched the keys on the computer board that started the ship in for the final pass.

Green dots formed behind the *Preceptor* on the vidscreen display. Norlin hoped they realized they were going to their deaths. Then, all thoughts of other ships vanished. He was too busy dealing with the Kindarians.

Lasartillery fired until the lasing tubes melted and the half-silvered mirrors vaporized. When the lasers died, he switched to the radiation cannon. Whenever a Kindarian target presented itself, he fired. The *Preceptor* drew the enemy like an electromagnet pulling iron filings, but Norlin didn't mind. He had a weapon to take out the enemy—and he did.

Barse flew into the control room.

"Cap'n, you got to stop using the radiation cannon. The switch is shot. Another blast will take out all our power. We'll be dead in space for hours while we regenerate!"

Norlin's pale violet eyes took in the vidscreen display, and he shook his head.

"We don't have any choice. They're on top of us."

"Run, dammit. We've got the power for that. Get us out of here!"

Norlin and Sarov came to the same conclusion using different techniques. Retreat was not what Norlin had come to do; Sarov discovered that one final firing of the radiation cannon was possible and would use less energy than fleeing.

Norlin triggered the radiation cannon.

The internal systems went down, plunging the ship into complete darkness. Even the soft, persistent hiss of the magnetic fans moving ionized air currents through life support died.

The cruiser drifted along its last vector, dead in space.

* * *

"I cannot return to the palace," Oloroun said. "Tidzio knows I have aided you."

"That's the least of our worries," Grendel said. "Where do we run?" He looked around the levitrain platform. The control room blinked and flashed the approach of a train.

"The train," Trahnee said. "We stop the train. We can go anywhere on Earth in a matter of hours."

"It's a start," admitted Grendel. He worked on the controls. "I'm not sure how this works. It might stop the train. If it does, we can be on the other side of the world in an hour. Even that won't be far enough. We need to get off-world fast."

Trahnee said nothing. She regretted that Pier Norlin wasn't here to help her. She missed his incisive tactical sense. He might not be genhanced, but he had a talent for planning that few others shared. If the minor coup she planned was to succeed, they needed clever—and new—tactics.

"There," said Oloroun. "Train comes and slows, stops!"

The train dropped on its superconducting field and came to a halt at the platform. Trahnee and Grendel rushed forward as a passenger door opened.

Grendel snarled and fired his laser rifle. Twin beams of potent energy burned him in half. Trahnee looked at the corpse of her co-conspirator, stunned at the suddenness of his death.

"You are a prisoner, Trahnee," came Chamberlain Tidzio's mocking voice. "Do you think we allow such easy entry to the palace? Emperor Arian is unharmed."

"You do not see me, Tidzio," she started to say, putting the full power of her genhanced talent into her command. The words jumbled in her throat. She tried to move, to run, to keep her eyelids from drooping. The humming of the paralysis field told her that Tidzio had come prepared. She dropped to her knees, then toppled onto her face.

The last thing she saw before darkness washed through her consciousness was Grendel's left foot and the charred stump just above it where it had been attached to his leg.

* * *

Power returned slowly. When the lights winked back on in the control room, Norlin jumped; the ship's cat was curled up in his lap. Neutron looked up, his green eyes glowing in the wan light. Norlin petted the animal automatically as he studied the few displays coming up inside his command helmet.

"We're almost back to minimum," said Chikako. "I've got a com-link with the *Subterfuge*. That's the only battleship left able to com with us."

Norlin waited for the vidscreen to return before he spoke with the *Subterfuge*'s captain. The view that popped up made him grin. No red dots remained. A few green ones moved around Epsilon Eridani II, but what thrilled him most was the sight of the planet's space station. If the Kindarians had won, the station would have been totally destroyed. Its presence spoke out as a clear signal of victory for the Empire Service.

"Status," Norlin asked his own crew after hearing the report from the other ship's captain.

"Coming up. There are more of us left than show on the vidscreen," said Chikako. "A score or more of our ships were erroneously listed as dead. We've got fully forty percent left, although none is in full fighting trim."

"How does it look planetside?"

"They took heavy damage," reported Sarov, "but they are still alive. Moving the Death Fleet in close saved all of us. The Kindarians would have wiped us out then concentrated on the planet. Getting caught between the planet-based weapons, the space station and us did them in."

Norlin played with the controls and got a vidscreen picture of their captive. He hadn't moved during the battle. Norlin wondered what thoughts ran through the spider-like creature's brain.

"Got the com-link re-established between planet and all units of our fleet," said Chikako. "Liottey's working overtime getting us back into fighting trim. Without serious drydock time, he's not going to succeed, but we might be able to fire lasers and hobble about."

Norlin punched up the combination that brought the *Subterfuge*'s captain, Ten Gettar, onto the vidscreen. The tired, gaunt man smiled when he saw Norlin.

"Congratulations, Admiral, we've won a decisive victory. We didn't even know such a fleet existed until you brought the news to us. I must apologize for doubting you."

"The battle has just started," said Norlin. "The Black Nebula holds their homeworld. We're going to destroy them from inside out, just as they tried to do to us."

"There's no doubt they would have gone on to Earth if they had been successful here," the battleship's captain agreed. "Such savagery. It makes the emperor's war games look tame."

"There's no substitute for real combat," said Norlin. "My com officer is in touch with a few of the other ships, but we cannot go on to the Black Nebula in this condition. Can we refit at the EE space station?"

"It was designed for fleet work," Captain Gettar said. "You need to authorize it. You're fleet admiral, after all."

Norlin shook himself. He had not gotten used to the position—and the power that came with the title.

"There won't be any trouble, will there?"

"You're referring to the sordid business with Galimeer?" The captain shook his head. "There aren't many genhanced officers willing to follow his orbit, not after *this* battle."

"You're genhanced," Norlin said. Something about the man's bearing hinted at arrogance and contempt for those who lacked his genetically altered attributes.

"I am, but you won't get any trouble from me. I know tactics—and I know when I see someone better than me at them. You've defeated two of the emperor's finest, after all."

Norlin knew he referred to not only Galimeer but the captain of the *Negation*. It was a pity important units of the ES fleet had needed to be destroyed to whip the others into shape.

"How many ships can we expect to get back into full battle condition?" he asked.

"I've got officers doing damage estimates now. Preliminary guesses run to about forty. The dry docks at the space station will require a month or so to refit."

"Forty," mused Norlin. "Is that enough to make a good foray into the Black Nebula?" he asked Sarov.

"I'll check it. We'll need a full load of missiles. Make sure they've got programmables—we've got to put the Kindarian ship signatures into their memory for maximum efficiency. Mostly, I need to know the classes of ships comprising that forty. Forty battleships would be good, if impossible, but with only forty scouts…" Sarov shook his head.

"We're working on the number of ships we'll need," Norlin told Captain Gettar. "What of the Death Fleet? Did you or someone on-planet track their stragglers?"

"They took off in all directions. They ran without orders," the captain said. "We defeated them soundly. Unless they have a predetermined rendezvous point, they're scattered all over the Orion Arm."

"They don't," Norlin said. "They've never been so completely routed before. They've left fractions of their fleet and sent the rest on to destroy other worlds, but this is the first time we've met their full force and defeated it."

"You've had some experience with them, haven't you, Admiral?"

"I'll have my com officer microburst you my report on what's been happening in the colonies. You'll find it instructive."

"Shall I tend to the repair work?" asked Gettar. "For three years, I was ordnance commander back on Earth."

"Do it," ordered Norlin. "I've got to set the preliminary battle simulations to see if our force will be adequate to handle the Kindarians on their home ground."

"They'll be without a fleet. That makes it easier," Gettar said.

"Bad news—this is only about a quarter of their total fleet. We got this from a prisoner we took."

"He was lying!" The genhanced officer looked outraged. "No world can space a fleet four times this in size!"

Norlin shrugged. He didn't know if their prisoner had lied or simply repeated propaganda he thought was the truth.

"We've got to plan for the worst. Their depredations on our worlds have to be stopped. Cutting them off at their homeworld seems the quickest way of doing it, since we don't know where the rest of their force is, but there might be other options that will serve the same purpose."

"What has Emperor Arian done by way of planning?"

"We're it," Norlin said. He watched outrage form on the captain's face. "Get to work. Give the *Preceptor* priority status. I might have to do some exploring."

"You're going after the stragglers?"

"I want a complete com blackout between Epsilon Eridani and Earth. Any problem enforcing that?"

"Some. The people on-planet will protest, but they might not have much com back home."

"Keep this quiet. If necessary, I'll brief the emperor on our victory—and the forthcoming expedition to the Black Nebula."

"Understood, Admiral." The vidscreen went black.

"What are you planning?" came Barse's gravel-voiced question. "You're not thinking of chasing them down?"

"No," Norlin said. "After we repair the ship, we're returning to Earth."

"Trahnee?" asked Barse.

Norlin nodded. He had bad feelings about leaving her. A week's shift back to Earth wouldn't delay the expedition to the Black Nebula, since it would take more than a month for the other ships to be returned to fighting trim.

Barse shook her head and left. Sarov and Miza dutifully turned back to their boards, trying not to show their displeasure. Norlin didn't care if they liked it or not. He was captain of the *Preceptor*—he was *admiral* of the Empire Service fleet. Captains and admirals commanded. It was that simple.

He wished it was so simple he could decide where his duty really lay.

# Chapter Fourteen

Trahnee sat in the pit and tried to ignore the excrement thrown down on her by Emperor Arian's courtiers. Tidzio goaded them on. She knew he had arranged for this further humiliation because she had not agreed to the debasement he insisted she endure. To fight in the emperor's arena meant slow death. She saw no reason to make a spectacle of it.

A week earlier—or was it longer?—she had been put into the arena with a slavering beast. She simply stood and waited for it to rip her apart. It had proven to be a hologram, not a real creature. Tidzio had been furious at her lack of response.

Trahnee had seen how the spectators wallowed in the fear shown by the victim. If the prisoner fought, it meant little. The defeat of a real beast only meant the introduction of another and another and another until the amusement ended in death for the human victim. She saw no reason to feed their sick expectations. Better to simply surrender and rob them of their tawdry show.

That had allowed her to live this long, even if it was in such filth and degradation. Tidzio wanted a true spectacle, and she refused to provide it.

"Give me a decent death, Trahnee," Tidzio yelled down. He wore huge muffs over his ears to filter the effects of her genhanced voice. "Fight, rebel, struggle, die nobly! You are too good to live in such debasement."

She refused to let him bait her. She sat with her head bowed, the fecal matter raining down on her.

Beside her, Oloroun had dug a small cavity in the wall and huddled there, constantly growling deep in his throat. For reasons known only to Tidzio, the Prothasian had been spared most of the indignity he had heaped so lavishly on her. Trahnee didn't care; she was beyond that.

Tidzio yelled down at her, "You'll do as I want. It may not be today or tomorrow, but you will! The emperor demands it! Your vanity will yield to Emperor Arian's desires!"

Trahnee wasn't sure that being left alone wasn't worse than the unwanted attention. Oloroun said nothing as he rolled himself into a tight furred ball and cowered in his cavity. She looked up and saw only patches of white cloud as they drifted across the dome of the blue sky.

"Pier," she said softly. "Pier…"

✳ ✳ ✳

"This is risky, Cap'n," warned Tia Barse. "If I read them right, they're not going to like you tearing off with the fleet and keeping them in the dark."

Norlin nodded agreement.

"Tidzio wanted control over me," he admitted. He told her how the emperor's chamberlain had tried to imprison her and Liottey on Star's End.

"The miserable little runt!" the engineer raged. "He couldn't do it. There's not enough men this side of Earth who could keep me from the *Preceptor*!"

"Trahnee and I took care of that."

"Distilled water?" scoffed Barse. "You should have used real poison. Get rid of the dwarf once and for all."

"What are we likely to encounter if we sneak in toward Earth?" he asked Chikako.

The com officer glanced over her shoulder.

"It's going to be hard to get in undetected—they've got everything stretched to the limit. Word of the battle must have reached there from AlphaCent by now."

"Can we do it?" demanded Norlin. "I don't want to alert every scout ship—and Tidzio—of our arrival if we can avoid it."

"It might be easier to blast a few of them from space," said Sarov. "There's no interchange among the units. A sorry state for defense, if you ask me. We can punch a hole anywhere through their defensive array and dart directly inward."

"We don't destroy any ships, unless it's the only way we can contact Trahnee."

"She's not worth it, Cap'n." Barse's colorless eyes bored into his. "She's genhanced. Given the chance, she'll sell you out. Wait and see. All she wants is the approval of the other genhanced."

"Perhaps she will betray me," said Norlin. "That's my business."

"It matters to everyone on this ship," corrected Barse. "We're a team, we're shipmates. We're a *crew*. If we don't look out for each other, who will?"

"I may have saved you and Liottey from the chamberlain, but you don't have to save me from Trahnee," he said.

Silence fell as the com and tac officers worked the cruiser through the sensor net deployed around the solar system. Norlin was fascinated by the way Chikako and Sarov worked together. Without being told, he would launch a decoy missile, and she would jam a sensor for only a few minutes to give them enough time to slip past a detector post. Entering the solar system at an angle to the plane of the ecliptic made their job easier—there were fewer sensors per cubic light-hour. They managed to penetrate the orbit of Mars before being challenged by a cruising picket ship.

"Admiral Norlin in the Empire Service flagship *Preceptor*," he answered immediately. "Go to code yellow, code sapphire, code nineteen-zero."

"What's that do for us?" asked Barse.

"If he obeys, it cuts him off from reporting for one hour. It's not much time but will have to do. I told him we're on a secret mission from the emperor and need the time to complete our assignment."

"He won't call the palace to verify, will he?" asked Liottey over the com-link. "That would give away the show."

"He's a sub-commander or lower. He might be a junior lieutenant. No junior officer contacts the emperor directly. We're still more than thirty light-minutes out, too. That adds to our margin considerably."

"You're right, Captain," said Chikako. "He's flashed his agreement to your coded message. We'd better make the most of it—I'm picking up heavy armament coming into the field. Two battleships and a cruiser and maybe more out of Mars."

Norlin fumed. The emperor had told him he had the pick of the solar system's defensive fleet. Arian had lied—these three ships proved that—but it was nothing he hadn't suspected. The emperor wasn't likely to commit the entire fleet to an invasion of a light-years-distant nebula and leave himself unprotected. Trahnee wasn't the only one trying to overthrow the current regime.

"Commercial vid pickup, Captain," said Chikako. "You'd better take a look at it. We might have returned just in time."

Norlin frowned. Sarov began arming the genius missiles and running checks on the forward lasartillery battery. He turned to the vidscreen and watched the smarmy announcer for several seconds before the import of the man's words sank in.

"They're going to torture Trahnee to death—and they're doing it on public trivid!" he raged.

"Not quite, sir," said Chikako, still listening intently. "She's been condemned as a traitor, attempted assassination, betrayal of the realm—the usual gibberish. She's refused to do something. I don't understand this part."

Norlin did. The emperor had ordered her to fight to the death, and she had refused. He read the unspoken message well enough. She would be harassed until she agreed to die on vid-camera.

"There wasn't any mention where she was being kept," Norlin called to Chikako. He looked toward her station and saw the circuitry woven through her scalplock ablaze as she received and sent messages. He waited until the furious activity died down before asking, "Do you know where Trahnee is?"

"Pinpointed," the com officer said. "Near the palace, less than a kilometer to the west. Near a levitrain station—and a major base. Captain, there are enough soldiers there to guard a million prisoners, much less Trahnee."

Norlin laughed without humor. He hadn't fought his way through the Kindarian fleet to be thwarted by a few ground-gripper soldiers who owed their allegiance to a stunted, power-mad chamberlain. His fingers lightly tapped in a sequence that flashed to Sarov's board.

"Are you sure?" the burly tac officer asked. "I'll do it, but this is treason."

"Thank you. Do it." Norlin took a deep breath, then hit the com-link that patched him through to everyone aboard the *Preceptor*. "I've ordered Sarov to use the lasartillery on a ground base so that I can attempt to rescue Trahnee. This is an act of rebellion, although it is not aimed at the emperor personally and is not an attempt to depose him. If you choose not to take part, let me know; I'll see you reach Star's End safely. You can tell the authorities you tried to stop me but were overpowered."

Barse snorted.

"Hell, Cap'n, we could stop you if we wanted. I've been telling you we should kick ass here for some time. I don't much like that genhanced…woman, but she's doing what I want to see done. Let me get to the engine room before you dip down."

The engineer trotted off before he could thank her. Liottey relayed his desire to stay aboard. Sarov had already agreed by arming the missiles. Chikako Miza was the last to acknowledge. She apologized for being too tied up in her communications to respond more quickly.

"We're a crew, Captain," she said. "Even if one of us goes off on a corkscrew orbit, we're a crew. You want a path plotted to go down in a shuttle?"

"During lasartillery bombardment," he decided.

He slipped from the command chair and motioned to Sarov to take the conn. Norlin wondered if he would ever see the familiar insides of the *Preceptor* again. Even with heavy bombardment from space, that was a huge military base. Getting to the ground, finding Trahnee and returning safely with her would be difficult.

It might even be impossible.

Before entering the shuttle, he packed what gear he thought would prove useful. Never having engaged in such sedition before, he wasn't sure what he could use and what would only be excess weight. The laserifle was a definite inclusion; he slung a spare over his shoulder next to the small satchel containing electronic homing equipment for Chikako to trace him.

"Good hunting, Cap'n," Barse said as he climbed into the ship's small secondary shuttle.

He would be exposed on his way down; only the covering fire from the *Preceptor* would protect him. Even with his best piloting, the tiny shuttle had limited maneuverability.

Norlin closed his eyes, took a deep breath, then concentrated on the controls. When Sarov jettisoned the shuttle, he was ready

Air screamed past the hull immediately; he had been shot directly into the upper reaches of the Earth's covering blanket of atmosphere. On the shuttle's tiny vidscreen he saw the *Preceptor* open up with lasartillery and selected missiles. Some missiles produced sensor-confusing readings. Others blew circling hyperwing patrols out of the sky. The lasartillery concentrated on the ground base filled with soldiers.

Norlin didn't like this part of it, but *he* hadn't imprisoned Trahnee and countless others. It was time someone stood up to such tyranny—and he was the one to do it.

He fought the shuttle through heavy buffeting, both from turbulence caused by the *Preceptor*'s lasartillery ionizing the atmosphere around him and from ground fire. After an eternity, he brought the shuttle to a shuddering halt on the ground. He glanced at the rear view from tiny vidcams on the hull. A shallow trench more than a kilometer long marked his location. He would have to finish his rescue quickly—a blind man could find the shuttle.

Norlin checked the outer hull and saw that the poisonous gases released during the fiery descent had dissipated. He popped the hatch and jumped clear. Heat boiled off the hull, raising blisters and beads of sweat on his exposed skin. He dashed in the direction Chikako had identified as being the holding area for prisoners.

He came to a halt and stared. The entire vicinity had been blown to hell and gone. He touched the com-link at his belt.

"Sarov, did you raze it?"

"We watched the soldiers do it, Captain," came the dour tac officer's voice in his ear. "They are going berserk. There might be a mutiny underway, though it is impossible to tell from up here."

"Trahnee, where's Trahnee?" he demanded.

Chikako answered. "There's an arena two klicks sunward. The size of the crowd indicates some type of festivity. I've got evidence of Emperor Arian being there, too."

He didn't ask what evidence she had seen. He started dog-trotting in the indicated direction, cursing as he ran. At this speed, he was less than ten minutes away.

The spare laserifle slammed hard into his back with every stride, but Norlin didn't regret having brought it. If he had to fight his way through half the Empire Service soldiers on Earth, he'd need it—and maybe more.

Out of breath and cursing even more volubly, he came to a high fence circling the arena in either direction.

"You're there, Captain," came Chikako's calm voice. "Right on target. We're getting a good picture through the CCDs. It doesn't look good. A figure that might be Trahnee is at the edge of a large open area—it's a sacrifice of some sort. Definition isn't good enough to decide if the brown speck next to her is Olor-oun. The computer guesses that it is."

"Ahead?"

"I've put a homer into the com-link. Just follow the beep."

Norlin swung around and immediately picked up the signal from the unit. He started toward the spot where the beeping grew in frequency. A guard stopped him almost immediately.

"Only the emperor's personal party is allowed through," the guard said.

"Admiral Norlin to see Chamberlain Tidzio," he said. Norlin decided not to invoke the emperor's name—others might do that to obtain illicit entry. The expression on the guard's face reflected shock at the mention of the chamberlain.

"Wha—"

He got no further. Norlin swung the laserifle around and caught him squarely under the chin. The man's head snapped back, and he sank to the ground. Norlin spent the next three minutes subverting the automatic defenses at the gate. Only then did he rush into the heart of the arena.

He slowed to a fast walk as the corridors became crowded. No one was inclined to question him or ask why he carried two laserifles. He stopped and stared at the crowd when he came into the open.

Thirty thousand or more spectators lined the sloping banks of seats in the partially covered arena. Locating the emperor's box was simple. He found the flowing purple streamers snapping in the brisk breeze blowing through the arena, powered by fans aimed to produce the effect. Behind assassin-proof glasteel panels sat Emperor Arian.

Norlin pushed through the crowd and leaned over the rail circling the amphitheater. Trahnee, Oloroun and a dozen others stood three meters below him, nervously awaiting…what?

"Trahnee!" he shouted.

His voice was drowned out by the crowd's roar. Across the arena came a dozen armed soldiers.

"Supporting fire," ordered Norlin into his com-link. "I'll need help, lots of it."

"Lasartillery fire, aye," came Sarov's measured response.

Norlin unlimbered one laserifle and rested it on the railing. He turned on the sighting spot and found the chest of an advancing solider. Not hesitating, he fired. The weapon roared and brought the soldier down.

The other soldiers around him scattered and dived. Norlin both applauded and cursed their expert training. Getting a sighting on a second soldier would be almost impossible now that he had lost the element of surprise.

"Pier!" cried Trahnee. "Don't try to rescue us. Run! You can't make it!"

He worried she might be right. He glanced toward the emperor's box and saw a steady stream of soldiers pouring out in both directions. It would take some time for them to make their way through the crowd, but he didn't doubt there were others who were much closer to him. He cast a quick look in both directions and saw the crowd melting away from him. He would be targeted quickly now.

"Take this!" He dropped his spare laserifle to her. She used it to hold the soldiers inside the arena at bay.

He kept up a steady fire, designed more to force people away than to injure, as he tried to find a way down into the arena…and failed. No stairs, no ladder, nothing.

He grunted as he jumped onto the railing. He hesitated for a moment then dropped. The three-meter fall almost disoriented him. He hit and tried to roll but caught a foot under him. He went down heavily, knocking the air from his lungs.

Small, furry hands grabbed at his fallen laserifle. Oloroun turned it upward and cindered two soldiers trying to fire down at them.

"You're good with that," gasped out Norlin. "Keep it—and keep using it." He pulled his laser pistol and struggled to stand.

Trahnee came over to him.

"You shouldn't have come. Tidzio will kill us both now."

"Let him try." Norlin touched the com-link at his belt. "Sarov, we can use more supporting fire."

The arena erupted in flame as the heavy forward lasartillery batteries opened up. They had replaced one lasartillery nodule with the captured Kindarian radiation cannon, but the other three raked the arena and stands. Norlin swallowed hard at the sight of so many dying. Even more would be trampled as panic spread.

"Coming for you, Cap'n," called Tia Barse. "Get out in the center of the arena. It's the only place I can be sure of setting down."

He looked up and saw the *Preceptor*'s larger shuttle flying in a tight circle above them. Landing would be almost impossible.

"Stay here until she gets lower," he told Trahnee.

The others with her bolted and ran. The soldiers on the arena floor cut them down as they fled. Only Trahnee and Oloroun remained alive after another three minutes.

The trio—human, genhanced and Prothasian—fought side-by-side to keep the soldiers at a distance. Inexorably, sheer numbers wore them down. A laserifle bolt almost removed Norlin's left arm; Trahnee had to beat out the flames as his uniform tunic caught fire. His arm hung useless at his side.

"There!" he cried after about ten minutes of firefight. "There's Barse. Get to the middle of the arena and hope she can bring the shuttle in."

Sarov increased the heavy barrage. Norlin got to the center of the arena and used his pistol to dig a shallow trench. He, Trahnee and Oloroun dropped into it, as much to protect themselves from the soldiers' fire as from the hot exhaust of the descending shuttle's engines. Backwash set fire to the rest of his tunic. Norlin awkwardly ripped it free and tossed it aside.

"She did it!" cried Trahnee. "Barse got down."

"Getting out isn't going to be any easier."

They ran for their lives. On all sides, soldiers poured in. The hull of the shuttle withstood the fire of individual laserifles. Ten had mattered little. Hundreds now focused on the blunt prow. For all the atmospheric friction the vessel could endure, it would puncture soon from the intense firepower bearing on it unless they took off quickly.

"Welcome aboard. Next stop, orbit," greeted Barse. She didn't even wait for Norlin to cycle the airlock shut. She kicked in the powerful engines, swung in a wide circle and took out most of the attacking troops. "Hate this. They don't deserve to die just because they're doing their duty," she grumbled.

"Get us the hell out of here!" Norlin shouted.

Barse didn't hear him. She wore headphones that linked her to the *Preceptor*. Her lips moved as she directed Sarov's lasartillery fire. Only when the end of the arena had been reduced to smoldering ruin did she slam full power to the shuttle's engines.

They blasted forward so fast that Norlin, who wasn't yet strapped down in his efforts to see that Trahnee and Oloroun were cared for, was slammed hard into a bulkhead. Darkness fell. He vaguely remembered hearing Barse's voice over his comlink asking for a long blast from the radiation cannon.

The next thing he was conscious of was Trahnee bending over to kiss him aboard the *Preceptor*.

"Get us out of here," he mumbled. "Back to Epsilon Eridani. I can use the rest before we invade the Black Nebula."

Black space again engulfed him.

# Chapter Fifteen

**W**e are in the middle of hell, Captain," said Sarov. "We are trying to counter everything they can throw at us. It is not easy, since their equipment is better than ours. Star's End is especially bad for us. They have got the lasartillery to blow us out of space—and the only thing stopping them is how we dodge."

"Get the radiation cannon working," said Barse. "Give 'em a taste of their own photon wash."

"No!" Norlin startled himself with his vehemence. "We're not here to do battle with the empire."

He heaved a deep sigh. He had rescued Trahnee and Oloroun. *That* had been his sole reason for returning to Earth. Getting back to Epsilon Eridani and resuming command of the ES fleet was paramount.

"Tidzio will have contacted the fleet by now," pointed out Chikako Miza. "He's got scout ships that can make the trip in half the time it takes us. Inverse square on the speed, remember. A ship half our size can travel the ten-point-eight light-years in a quarter the time it takes us. Make that…hmm, taking delays into account—three days."

"They might send a message packet," suggested the furry Oloroun. "Tidzio always all the time is sending them around the empire."

"The report of our treason will be there waiting for us," Norlin said, resigned. "When Tidzio found out he'd lost contact with the fleet before we left for Alpha Centauri, he sent out ships. Count on it."

Trahnee sat to one side of the control room, Oloroun curled up beside her. The genhanced woman and the Prothasian talked in low tones. Norlin surveyed the vidscreen and saw that Star's End was orbiting out of position. That gave them a few hours grace before they had to decide whether to shift this close to Earth or fight.

His allegiance to the empire had dwindled considerably, but he still considered himself an officer sworn to uphold its unity. The contradiction of an officer fighting the emperor was not lost on him.

"What happened with the coup?" he asked Trahnee.

"Tidzio's intelligence network made a mockery of Grendel's forces."

"Grendel?"

"Code name Eagle," Trahnee explained. "Grendel's every move was relayed to Tidzio. We were captured without much effort." She wiped away a tear forming at the corner of her eye. "I needed Bo. He always made it so much better." She looked up. "You should have been there. Together we could have overthrown Arian. It was so close. I felt it!"

"There're more important concerns," he said. "The Kindarians, for instance."

"I know," she said. "But this is important, too. Oloroun understands."

The bear creature's head bobbed up and down.

"They do nasty things to us. Hurt me. Hurt Trahnee bad." He raked the air with his gleaming claws. "Treat us like animals. *They* are animals."

"Sarov," asked Norlin, "is there any chance the emperor and Tidzio were caught in your barrage?"

"Little chance," the dour tac officer said. "We concentrated on the arena, but all our heavy missiles were intercepted. We did not soften the base adequately. They had firepower to stop us."

"The space station powered up fast, too," said Chikako. "They let us have our way for several minutes—I think we took them by surprise. When it became obvious what we were doing, they opened up on us with their lasartillery. They've got powerful defenses."

Norlin idly ran a battle scenario through his computer to check how the Earth would fare against the full Kindarian Death Fleet. The computer beeped, not able to give a definitive answer. It would have been a close battle. The armaments were in place; the deciding factor, as always, lay in the organic brains behind the computers. The genhanced officers might turn the tide if the aliens attacked.

But the Kindarians retreated now. His fleet had met theirs in the Alpha Centauri system, defeated them soundly at Epsilon Eridani and now prepared to carry the war to their worlds.

"Missiles coming up from the surface," barked Sarov. "We are running low on defensives."

Norlin heard the crackling of the lasartillery as the weapons charged and fired forward of the bridge. Everything to the stern was cargo space, quarters or engine compartment. He checked power levels and proximity to Earth.

"Shift for Epsilon Eridani. The course is laid in. The geodesics are pulled away from us by the Earth's gravity well, but we've got no choice. If we stay and fight, we're going to lose."

"Receiving a message from Tidzio demanding our surrender. Is there a reply?" asked Chikako.

"No reply, dammit," Norlin said.

Tidzio's message showed that he still lived. That meant the emperor had survived, also. Tidzio would have been too busy consolidating his position to contact them if Emperor Arian had died.

"Do we have to shift this close to Earth? It'll throw the engine alignment off, Cap'n," came Barse's worried voice over his headphones. She had listened in to everything being said from the control room. "We might not be able to drop back precisely."

"Get us to Epsilon Eridani. We'll worry about accuracy at the other end." He looked at the vidscreen and frowned. Space was boiling around them. Too many lasers, too many missiles—and all seeking them.

"We'll get there, but I won't be held responsible for any flight error."

Norlin gave one last look at the white-clouded, blue-skyed water world that was mankind's birthplace. The ship took a side-step then initiated the gut-wrenching shift for the light-years-distant Epsilon Eridani system.

He said to Oloroun, "We'll find you a place to stay. Ask First Officer Liottey."

"Good. I thank you for such refuge. Tidzio would have killed me bad. You are good. We will work together for mutual benefits."

Norlin shook hands with the Prothasian then put his arm around Trahnee. They had a great deal to talk over before they arrived at Epsilon Eridani.

✳ ✳ ✳

"Twenty light-minutes!" wailed Barse. "My engines are ruined. There's no alignment. I warned you, Cap'n. We're twenty goddamn light-minutes off-target!"

"We'll survive," he said. "When we get into dry dock, you can reset the crystals in a few days."

"Weeks!" protested Barse. "I need weeks to do it right. We can't shift five thousand or more light-years to the Sagittarius Arm with faulty alignment. We…we might end up adrift in intergalactic space! Twenty light-minutes off! I've never been that far off. Ever."

Liottey had worked hard to repair the internal damage the *Preceptor* had taken as they fled from Earth. Sarov and Miza had done what they could but were unable to venture outside to repair the equipment and lasartillery nodules on the hull while they were in shift space. They had left that until they reached the Epsilon Eridani dry dock facility.

"I'm receiving com you might want to hear, Captain," said Chikako. Her scalplock blazed with the communications traffic flowing across her board and through her circuits. "There's been a mutiny."

"Tidzio's scout reached here before we did," he said, guessing the cause.

"*Preceptor*, come in. Commander Lu of the cruiser *Feign*."

Norlin waited for the message. Although they drove at full thrust toward Epsilon Eridani II, the speed of light prevented easy com. A question took almost a half-hour to answer.

"…Captains Blane and Escobar responded to Chamberlain Tidzio's call for mutiny."

"Who are they?" Norlin asked Chikako.

Chikako got a vacant look in her eyes before answering.

"Midget battleship and another nova-class cruiser. I don't know their politics." She deferred to Trahnee on this.

The genhanced woman shook her head. She didn't know either of the spacemen.

Norlin returned to the message from Commander Lu.

"Eight other units rallied to their call for obedience to the emperor."

Norlin closed his eyes. Ten ships of the forty remaining to his tiny fleet had mutinied. Heaviness sank onto his shoulders and crushed him. How long had it been before the others had joined them? When would this Commander Lu tell him he was an outlaw and they awaited him for the court-martial?

"All were destroyed by the elements of the fleet remaining loyal."

Norlin sat upright, eyes wide in surprise.

"Lu and the others turned on ten of their comrades?"

"So it appears, Captain," said Chikako. "We'll be in better shape to communicate in a few hours."

"Send our regards and all that," he said, still not believing the majority of the fleet had supported him rather than the emperor—or Tidzio. "See if you can get some idea if this is a trap."

"I do not think so," said Sarov. "I have found plasma traces, enough to explain ten ships being destroyed."

"Keep a sharp watch," he said. Turning to Trahnee, he muttered, "Is it possible they chose to follow us? Was your instruction to them that powerful? It's been weeks since you spoke with them," he said after reflection. So much had happened. A trip to Earth, the fight to get Trahnee free, the trip back. So much.

"If they follow you, it's because of you, Pier, not me. My power over others fades as time flows. I need to reinforce constantly. Even then, I cannot efface a deeply held belief without great effort, and against other genhanced, well, they either know or sense my power and can circumvent it to some extent."

"We'll see," Norlin said, still unwilling to believe the ES fleet had been loyal to him rather than Emperor Arian.

\* \* \*

Sixteen hours later, Pier Norlin believed it. Commander Lu personally came aboard the *Preceptor* to greet him.

"It is a pleasure to meet you like this," Lu said. The man stood a head shorter than Norlin and had lank black hair that kept falling into his eyes. He bowed constantly and made Norlin think of a child's toy with a bearing broken.

"What happened? You sketched out the way Tidzio's message caused Blane and Escobar to revolt but…"

"There are many among the senior officers, all genhanced, who have been increasingly disturbed with the direction the empire has gone." Lu cleared his throat. "Stagnation is endemic. You, who are not even genhanced, led us to a real victory."

"We lost a sizable portion of the fleet."

"The Kindarians are worthy opponents," Lu said. "We analyzed your tactics and found in them the germ of brilliance. Emperor Arian proclaims only the genhanced can rule."

"I don't mean to be insulting, but many of the genhanced are incapable of anything but insane acts."

Lu solemnly said, "We know. Blane was such a case. Escobar followed Blane out of loyalty and not from any other reason. The rest of the fleet chose to prevent them from returning to Earth."

"Those weren't their orders," Norlin said. "They were supposed to destroy the *Preceptor*."

Lu bowed deeply.

"Of course. What other order could the chamberlain give? You threaten his carefully maintained order. You disprove the claim of incapacity for non-genhanced. You are a true hero."

Norlin started to argue. Trahnee cut him off.

"He is modest, Commander. He will disagree. That is all right. We know his true worth."

"We will follow you to the Kindarian homeworld, Admiral. We will triumph beside you."

"I can only thank you for your confidence, but the reality is more likely to be death for us all." Norlin clutched the sword Emperor Arian had given him. It had become a symbol to him of all that happened on Earth—and all that would happen.

He felt more confident holding it, as if this small token from a demented emperor gave him the authority he was so uncomfortable assuming on his own.

"You will triumph. I am genhanced. I *know* these things." Lu bowed again and left.

Norlin watched him shuttle back to the *Feign* and tried to put his feelings into words. He failed.

"You've given them hope, Pier," said Trahnee. "They'll follow you to the death because you inspire them. How many of the genhanced can make that claim?"

"I don't care. All they're likely to find in the Black Nebula is death. How many ships will be in our fleet?"

He looked to Sarov for the answer. The burly tac officer worked on the weapons board for a few seconds before flashing the response on the main vidscreen.

Norlin shuddered when he saw it. The Empire Service fleet had begun with a hundred ships. Defection, the Kindarians and other problems had reduced that number to only thirty to enter the Black Nebula.

"All ships are returned to fighting trim. They have reprogrammed their genius missiles for Kindarian ship signatures. We are ready to shift, Captain," reported Sarov.

"When Barse gives us the word that she's realigned our shift crystals, we'll start."

They began the four-month shift for the Black Nebula eight days later, a fleet of thirty against untold thousands in the Kindarian Death Fleet.

# Chapter Sixteen

Y ou're too tense, Pier," Trahnee said. "You're making yourself into a loser by your nervousness. Relax. Simply do what
you do best, and you will win."

Her words vibrated along his raw nerves. He jumped when
he felt her trying to use her persuasive powers on him.

"Don't do that," he snapped. "If anything goes wrong, I'll
be responsible for…"

"For what, Pier?" she asked gently.

"For the death of mankind. We have to stop the Death Fleet
from preying on our worlds. This is the most effective way to do
it. If I fail, there won't be a second attack, and billions will die.
Earth will die!"

"You are not alone," she said, her voice still low. "Victory or
loss does not mean life or death for the rest of humanity. Doesn't
the emperor share some of the credit—or blame?"

"Credit?" Norlin rubbed his eyes. He had been without sleep
for two days in preparation for shifting back into normal space.

He had done what he could to make sure the *Preceptor* was
ready. All internal systems worked to perfection. Barse and Sarov assured him the exterior equipment had been at maximum
when they left Epsilon Eridani. Oloroun spoke constantly of noble victory. None of this soothed Norlin's nerves.

Thirty against the Kindarian home world and countless ships and unknown defenses.

"Emperor Arian built this fleet, the one you lead. He is also to blame for not doing more, not responding when his colonies were being annihilated, for not even realizing how close the Death Fleet came to Earth."

"The empire's political infrastructure on Earth is dysfunctional," Norlin said, knowing that he understated the facts considerably. Earth was bankrupt morally, the emperor did not rule as much as indulge his whims, and those who did hold the empire together sought only to further their own schemes. The colony worlds had been cut adrift long ago, except for the levies required of them.

He tried to organize his thoughts. What was he saving? His fingers traced nervously over the hilt of the samurai sword Emperor Arian had given him. What did he get out of this expedition? It might eliminate the Kindarians as a menace, but to what end did *he* aspire? He didn't care for the position of admiral—the pressure on him was immense. Medals meant nothing to him. Power inside the Empire Service would always be denied him, since he wasn't genhanced. If he succeeded, he could seize that power permanently—but he didn't want it.

He looked at Trahnee. He wanted *her*. In spite of everything, he loved her. His gaze went to Sarov and Chikako. In his way, he loved them, too. Respect for their abilities, friendship—and love—bound them together.

The furred Prothasian Oloroun was a newcomer to the *Preceptor*'s crew but after the months in shift space, Norlin considered the small alien an integral part, too. The same applied to the engineer, Gowan Liottey and even the gas-producing ship's cat. They were a team. They belonged together.

What did he want for them and himself?

Norlin shook off the speculation. This excursion into the Black Nebula might resolve all his questions. None of them was likely to survive. The Kindarians had proven themselves implacable enemies, and, Norlin had to admit, entering their home territory with only thirty warships might be quick suicide.

"Ready to come out of shift," barked Tia Barse. "Power surge, aye. Here we go."

"All armaments ready, Sarov," Norlin ordered.

He took Trahnee's hand and gave it a quick squeeze. He laid the samurai sword aside, only to have Oloroun whisk it away to a special storage locker. Then the ship dropped back into normal space.

"We missed by light-years!" he protested.

"Not so, Captain," corrected Chikako. "The dust in the Sagittarius B-Two nebula is obscuring our sensors. I'm adjusting now. I have to filter out everything from cyanogen to formic acid and methylenimine. We've got a density of one-hundred-six particles per cubic centimeter and a temperature around thirty degrees K."

"Absorption, correct for the absorption," muttered Sarov, irritated at not getting clear signals for sighting. "I need to adjust for laser beam dispersion."

"I'm doing it." Chikako sounded as calm as if she ran a computer simulation problem rather than letting them vector along exposed to any attack from waiting Kindarian forces.

Norlin watched as Chikako keyed on the millimeter wave emission rather than depend on optical spectrum radiation. The dust cloud that was the nebula veiled completely what went on even a few light-hours away. He found himself marvelling at the way ultraviolet radiation failed to penetrate to the heart of the Black Nebula, whereas the dust didn't scatter the longer wave radiation.

Chikako adjusted their sensors and turned the vidscreen into a normal display, although the dust density in this portion of space reduced photon density to one-millionth of that they were used to.

"Got the other ships," she said, her scalplock circuitry flaring as she worked on adjusting their sensors. "All made it out of shift space. We're a fleet, we're in formation, and I've just transmitted my instrument corrections to them so we'll all be looking at the same thing."

"Keep a constant monitor up and down the spectrum," Norlin said. "We don't know how they fight in this murk."

The space around them was still hard vacuum, but the dust changed the way he would approach a planet—and fight in void.

"Picking up emanations from a star just ahead." Chikako let out a low whistle. "How did I ever miss *that*?"

Norlin looked at the image on the vidscreen. The dim outline of a planet wavered through the dust. Even using millimeter wave radiation, the reception was not good.

"No evidence of a space station guarding it," said Norlin. "What of engine exhaust?"

"Cannot track that in this mess," said Sarov. "The molecular hydrogen concentration is getting in the way of good analysis. I am picking up low-level energy emanations from the planet."

"No guardian spaceships," muttered Norlin. He didn't like swooping down and laying waste to a helpless planet, but the Kindarians had done just that to dozens of human-settled worlds. They had come looking for the Kindarian empire. Should he destroy outpost planets as they made their way to the center of the Black Nebula?

"Radio message, Captain," barked Chikako. "From the planet. They want to know who the hell we are."

"Commander Lu," he said, "take ten ships and hang back. Support us if necessary. Fleet, prepare for battle."

Norlin felt the adrenaline pumping fiercely through him. The planet didn't look like much, but it was the first of the Kindarian worlds. From the look of it, this was a throwaway outlying world, but it would test their fighting skills, their tactics, the mettle of the Empire Service crews.

Barse gave him the power he needed for a direct run at the planet. He ignored the warnings from his external sensors—they registered the outer fringes of a planet's atmosphere even though the *Preceptor* was in free space. The dust hindered and forced constant reassessment of their position.

"Got an orbit plotted for maximum bombardment damage, Captain," said Sarov.

Norlin glanced at it on the vidscreen, ran a quick verification through his computer then approved it. The plan was relayed to the other ships in their twenty-vessel attack force.

He watched the vidscreen as Chikako changed the view. When they achieved orbit and had readied the missile array, he shouted, "Stand down the missiles! Keep them at ready but don't fire." He passed the command along to the other ships. One light cruiser had already sent down a flight of atomic-tipped weapons.

"Look at the surface," Norlin said. "What do you make of it?"

"It's hard to distinguish details," said Trahnee. "But it doesn't appear there's anything on the world."

"There's one small source of radio signals," Chikako said. "The base is screaming bloody murder for dumping the nukes on their heads—the nearest landed about five hundred kilometers away."

"How many in the outpost?" asked Norlin, his keen eyes never leaving the vidscreen.

Barren, devastated land passed under them. It took ninety minutes to orbit the world. Except for the solitary Kindarian base, the planet was desolate.

"I've never seen such emptiness," said Trahnee. "The planet's surface is scarred and rocky, and no wonder. The atmosphere is barely breathable."

"It's as if they mined everything they could, then ripped away the soil and boiled the oceans. There's *nothing* down there."

"Sir, we're starting our second orbit. The other ships want to know what to do. Continue bombardment and remove the base or…I don't know what the alternative is."

"Break free. There's nothing worth destroying on-planet," he said. "The Kindarians have done it for us."

"Do you think this was a world colonized by a rival culture that the Death Fleet butchered on their way to our arm of the galaxy?"

Norlin didn't even notice who posed the question. It had already crossed his mind that the Kindarians had done their worst to this world.

"We might find allies if any natives are left. Those were definitely Kindarian signals, though." Chikako ran everything on her board into Norlin's computer for analysis. He purged it without examining it. He had faith in her judgment.

"The one station is all there is on the world." He came to his decision. "Lu, send in one missile targeted to Sarov's coordinates. One missile, multiple warheads, bracket the point, set for detonation after we've achieved a distance of twenty-five planetary radiuses."

"You're going to take out the relay station? Why? They can't harm us, even if they try reporting our presence," said Trahnee. "I have no love for the Kindarians, but there wasn't enough power to blast through a signal to another world."

"No!" protested Oloroun. "She is wrong. Do this to them. Do it! Destroy the enemy!" The little Prothasian had worked himself into a murderous rage against the Kindarians.

"The worlds are closely packed," said Chikako, her voice a point of calm in the emotional hurricane raging around Norlin. "The center of the Black Nebula is a birthing spot for suns—no life there at all. What we deal with lies on the fringe."

"You have more reason to hate them than I do, but…" Trahnee fell silent when she saw the steady track of the single missile Lu had fired. It arced inward as Norlin's segment of the fleet pulled out.

"We don't want nasty surprises later," he said. "They can't signal, but they might send an FTL packet to the homeworld."

"I watched for one to get a bearing and saw nothing," said Sarov.

"I was waiting, too. When they didn't alert their homeworld, I decided it was pointless letting them do it after we left."

"Never leave an enemy at your back," cut in Gowan Liottey. "Sound tactics."

Norlin studied the sensor readings Chikako and the other con officers had been accumulating. He locked in the proper vector and gave the order. In spite of the dust concentrations and the danger inherent in shifting, he had to reach the next world—the one most likely to hold a significant alien garrison.

He had to find their homeworld. He had to!

✳ ✳ ✳

"Something is wrong," fumed Pier Norlin. "We've examined six worlds in this damned dust bag of a nebula, and they're all like that!" He pointed to the world displayed on the control room's main vidscreen.

Craggy mountains stretched higher than the atmosphere, not because they were tall but because the atmosphere had been burned off. Combustion products hung low; the rest of the atmosphere had vanished into space. The surface stretched for millions of uninhabited hectares, useless for farming or manufacture or mining or anything. The scars where the Kindarians had performed brutal planetary surgeries remained—but Norlin was unable to decide what the aliens had taken.

One thing was clear—they had raped and left.

"They wanted something on those worlds," said Trahnee, "and they took it. They left the worlds hollow and devastated. Everything of value has been ripped away."

"There might not have been a single item they sought," said Barse, staring at the vidscreen over Norlin's shoulder. "The worlds might have given up everything they had, and the Kindarians moved on."

"No one rapes their own planets like this. Not even Emperor Arian is that stupid."

"Might not consider these their own worlds," pointed out Oloroun. "Might think of them as enemy worlds, like yours."

"They're aliens," said Trahnee, resting a hand on Oloroun's shoulder to reassure him that she did not consider him one with the Kindarians. "I have tried to speak with our prisoner to find out where their homeworld is in this murk, but he has withdrawn into a coma. It's surprising I was able to get the location of that first world from him."

"Catatonic from fear," grumbled Barse. "I threatened to put Neutron in with him."

Norlin waved her to silence.

"The worlds are all the same. Why? We're missing something."

Acid oceans stretched to the horizon as their vantage point shifted. Long dead, those seas lapped peacefully against their rocky shores. Hissing and sizzling took place wherever water touched stone and reacted chemically. In a few thousand years, the highly acidic ocean would have eroded the shores and become to a more neutral solution.

But of life or Kindarian outposts or any native intelligence on the world Norlin saw no trace.

The blare of an emergency signal spun him around in his command chair. Danger lights flashed, and his computer board went wild with the detection of a Kindarian vessel.

"What is it?" he asked Sarov. "It doesn't fit the signatures of anything I have in the computer—except for its exhaust. That's definitely a Kindarian fuel mix."

"It's big, Captain," said Chikako. "Fifty times the size of an empire battleship. It's an armored moonlet."

"At last, something to keep from losing our edge." Norlin had been worried the other ships in the fleet would turn careless after the string of uninhabited, uninhabitable worlds.

"Do not be too eager to go after it," Sarov said. "It is bristling with tubes I think are radiation cannon. Approaching it might be impossible without getting fried."

Norlin studied the readouts. He fumed that his view was obscured by the dust in the nebula. How had a race ever come to survive and prosper in such a murk? He tried to imagine how depressing it would be, going out at night, looking up and seeing only dark sky and a handful of stars.

"We go after it. Keep a tracer out to detect any com they have with their homeworld. We have to get a fix on it, or we'll wander around this morass forever."

"Aye, aye, Captain," Chikako Miza said without enthusiasm.

The lights dimmed in the *Preceptor* as the first blast from the armored planetoid's radiation cannon blazed across them. The flickering lights steadied. Norlin silently thanked Liottey for doing his job then turned to his own.

A dozen plans of attack flashed through his mind. He discarded them all.

"Put the planet between your ship and the Kindarian vessel," he ordered all his ships. "I don't want any unnecessary casualties. We're scouting now."

"Admiral Norlin, allow the *Feign* the honor of making the first run. We can destroy it."

"How, Commander?" asked Norlin. "Give my tac officer a full battle plan. Until then, do as ordered and interpose the planet between you and the Kindarian vessel."

Norlin's retreat forced the armored satellite to change its trajectory. As it did so, Chikako monitored it and got valuable information about its maneuverability, power source and even the number of enemy aboard.

"It'd take hundreds of organics to run something that large," she guessed. "I count forty radiation cannon. Even assuming computer sights, that requires ten fire control officers. From what we've seen, each battery has three additional crew."

He nodded. There wasn't any reason for the Kindarians to change their crew ratios from the larger ships used in the Death Fleet.

"Getting the *Feign*'s battle plan," said Sarov. "It looks good. They have a real virtuoso on the missile tubes. If she can lay down a volley like this…" He put the plan on Norlin's vidscreen. "…she can disable half their cannon on the first pass."

"Make that five ships, and they can destroy the armored planetoid," added Chikako.

"Let *Feign* try it," said Norlin. "Chikako, alert the other com officers to listen for a signal for help from the planetoid to Death Fleet units when we hit. I need time to restructure our position if they have reinforcements coming."

She nodded. They had to squeeze a response from the vessel or keep hunting.

"Commander Lu, your plan is authorized. Execute when you are ready."

"Heading out now, Admiral. Thank you!"

The *Feign* used the planet's gravity well to gather speed. Its trajectory spun it past the Kindarian satellite. At the precise point where it would do the most damage, an array of missiles blasted forth and blew off half the planetoid's rocky side.

"Couldn't be better," said Sarov. "They didn't get away unscathed, though. Two radiation cannon blasts hit them, if I read the instruments right."

"Only two," confirmed Chikako. "*Feign* is continuing on its orbit, no power, all presumed dead."

"What about the Kindarians?" pressed Norlin. "We need com between them and their base."

"Got it! A distinct break. I hope other ships picked it up. I can't be certain of the coordinates." Chikako waited for more than a minute before confirming that nineteen other ships in the fleet had intercepted the transmission. Within another two minutes, they had a triangulation fix on the plea for aid—directly to the Kindarian's homeworld, Norlin hoped.

"Take them," he ordered. "Stand off and use missiles."

"Sir, that will not work. Half their radiation cannon are down from *Feign*'s attack, but the rest of them can knock out missiles as they come in."

"Sarov, you worry too much. Line us up. Barse, give full power to our radiation cannon. Fire when they're in your sights, Sarov."

"Doing it, Captain," the tac officer said, as happy as Norlin had ever seen him.

The *Preceptor* shuddered as immense power flowed through the alien switching device and poured from the captured radiation cannon. The rocky walls of the hollowed-out asteroid melted away, exposing the metal sheeting beneath. Then this vanished.

The instant the enemy's firing paused, ES missiles began penetrating its defenses. Norlin tried to calculate which ship's missile caused the rapidly expanding ball of plasma when the armored planetoid exploded, but he couldn't assign proper credit. It might have been any of a half-dozen destroyers' genius missiles. He logged citations for all the attacking vessels and left it at that. There would be ample chances to win medals later.

"Nearest vessels, render aid to the *Feign*. Report when you can."

An hour after the Kindarian satellite's destruction, Lu and two survivors from the *Feign* were taken aboard the *Crusade*. Satisfied that all had been salvaged that could be, including the three crewmen who had died in the attack, Norlin plotted the course that would take the Empire Service fleet through the Black Nebula and drop them directly around the Kindarians' homeworld.

They couldn't do anything about the worlds that had been butchered, but they could stop the Kindarians from doing it again by sending out new elements of their Death Fleet.

"All ships, prepare to shift," Pier Norlin ordered. Hand trembling slightly, he launched toward the nearby star.

The battle of the Black Nebula had begun.

# Chapter Seventeen

"We've got them!" gloated Pier Norlin. "We have a direct line on their homeworld. We can take out the Kindarians and end this war once and for all."

"You sound too cheerful about it," said Trahnee. "It will not be easy. There are reasons to believe they will never surrender. Are you able to do as they do? Can you destroy an entire world, commit genocide on an entire race?"

"Are you trying to talk me out of this?"

Norlin ran his fingers over the keys of his tactical computer. The machine spat out a steady string of possible attack plans based on what they had already encountered. He knew they could win. A quick thrust at the Kindarians' home, and they would surrender. He knew it.

They had to!

"They've left their home undefended," Norlin said smugly. "The computer analysis suggests it. There's a damned good chance we'll meet only token resistance. We haven't encountered a real defensive force up to this point."

"So many ships in their Death Fleet," piped up Oloroun. "How can they defend when so many of them are out pillaging?"

"We've found nothing but ruined worlds," muttered Sarov. "I do not like that. It means they have stripped everything for… what?"

"You're not disagreeing with the computer analysis, are you, Sarov?" demanded Norlin.

"No, but the numbers can dance to many tunes. We might have neglected to input an important datum."

"We proceed at full," Norlin declared.

He issued the orders. The other ships keyed onto the *Preceptor*, and all shifted simultaneously.

Lights flared, and warning signs flickered on across his boards. Every exterior system on the cruiser protested the dense, hot material inside the nebula that blacked out so much of the visible light. Norlin tried to adjust the sensors to give a perfect view when they shifted back to normal space but failed. He'd had too little time to work on this problem.

He shrugged it off. Chikako had done an adequate job. He could operate by the flow of information crossing his heads-up display; he didn't need the vidscreen, although it helped him visualize the complex relationships between velocities of his fleet components and those of the Kindarian ships.

He turned back to running battle plans until the computer beeped in misery. He gave up.

"How long until we shift back?" he asked.

"Not long. The star density at the fringe of the Black Nebula is high. Inside the dust bag itself there are very few stars. Out here, we're seeing more than expected."

Norlin paced as he thought. The trip from Epsilon Eridani had been the farthest he had ever experienced in shift space. He had come a long way, both in experience and distance, from the picket ship he had manned when only a sub-lieutenant.

Admiral, he mused. He had reached exalted rank in the time most officers attained sub-commander. And it meant nothing. He had been lucky. Looking around and seeing Sarov and Chikako at work, he realized how lucky he was.

It was the team that was truly in command, not him personally.

Even as this thought crossed his mind, he realized how wrong it was. *He* was the captain. *He* commanded the *Preceptor*—and the fleet. The weight of that knowledge crushed him. Teams did not lead, individuals did.

"How long will we have to look around, Chikako?"

"After we shift back? Not long before the Kindarians detect us, if they're as alert as they usually are. I'd say less than five minutes. With such a large fleet entering their system, we'll have only their transmission time from detector to base. Given the technology in outer fringe detectors, we might not have even five minutes before they know we're not friendly."

Norlin worked frantically to finish an alternative attack plan. Just as the *Preceptor* dropped into normal space, the final components of the plan came out of the computer.

"Give it all to me," he said, sitting with his heads-up display set at full detail.

An eye-tearing array flashed in front of his face. He turned and moved and cocked his head from side to side to absorb it quickly.

"The only ships we're against are similar to the armored satellite," he said. "I make out thirty of them—they outnumber us by one. Do you check that, Sarov?"

"I do. There's no way to tell what support they might get from on-planet. I'm picking up anomalous power readings."

"Anomalous? How?" He switched the visuals on his display to those Sarov studied. "I don't understand. Those power leakage figures are far too low. This can't be their homeworld—not with a projection showing less than a tera-watt per year usage. That's lower than Earth's pre-space era."

"I cannot explain it," Sarov said. "We have to be cautious."

Norlin had never heard his tac officer ask for caution before. And what he intended to do was anything but circumspect.

"Split the fleet. Twenty-five to orbit and five to decoy away as many of the armored planetoids as possible. We're going directly in and take out the world."

"Split forces!" cried Sarov in outrage. "That is ridiculous! We need to protect one another. We cannot—"

"The order is sent," Norlin said. He didn't have time to argue with his officers. Teams didn't command, individuals did. And he realized he might be wrong.

The last battle plan had taken into account the planetoids they faced. He had to think of them as ships, but they were more—much more—and might easily vaporize the ships he had ordered to harass them. They lacked maneuverability, but they didn't need it inside the Kindarian home system. If the ES fleet turned and ran, he doubted any of the hollowed-out planetoids would pursue. Their function was to defend, not to rape and kill like the ships of the Death Fleet.

"Captain!" Sarov swung around, his face clouded with anger. Norlin's eyes locked on the tac officer's muddy brown ones. The feathery scars under Sarov's left eye turned a fiery red, but he turned back to his board and began working to fit the Preceptor and the other ships into the attack matrix.

Norlin didn't have time to explain his change in tactical direction to the man. He saw the thirty armored planetoids and knew that support from Kindar would make the approach disastrous if he failed for even an instant to keep his ships in position. His skill as commander-in-chief was too limited.

"They're using their radiation cannon early this time," came Chikako's calm voice. He wondered if anything ever upset her. "They've got to get the range first. Sighting at more than fifteen light-minutes is almost impossible."

"Barse? How are power levels? Are we ready?"

"Fire anything you want, Cap'n," came the engineer's excited voice. "I just tied down the cat. Neutron says to give 'em hell!"

"For the ship's cat, I'll do it," Norlin said, smiling wryly.

The vidscreen became a confused mass of red and green lines. Norlin reduced the details and was still confused by the movement. His twenty-five-ship fleet was already out of control—the com scrambling used by the Kindarians was more than a match for his officers' ability to penetrate. He had considered keeping a laser com-link among the ships, but that was impractical. Better to give each ship a mission and turn it loose.

"Just burned out the sensors on one of the planetoids," said Sarov. "They were sighting on us, and I pumped an optical laser ray back down their beam."

Norlin nodded, even though the others couldn't see the motion inside his helmet. Damage reports from Liottey began to pile up. The first officer and Barse worked with their robot crews to repair, but the nearer flashes of the Kindarian radiation cannons began to damage the lesser-protected circuits on the *Preceptor*.

"Missiles away," he said, launching a volley.

The genius missiles found the Kindarian planetoid signatures and locked onto them. Most of the missiles were destroyed before they had travelled half the distance to the armored planetoids. Norlin didn't care. The missiles kept the aliens busy and let his small fleet work its way inside their defensive ring.

The aliens might have the firepower, but the genhanced officers commanding the Empire Service ships proved their worth. Norlin marveled at the twists and turns and feints and outright daring shown by the other vessels.

The *Preceptor* went through paces no less devious, but he lacked the unassailable sureness the genhanced enjoyed. He fleetingly wondered if their true advantage lay in their ego rather than in any true ability.

Then he had no time for anything but fighting. The *Preceptor* found itself sandwiched two of the armored planetoids.

"They've got us in a crossfire," warned Chikako. "There's no com between them. They *know*."

Norlin piloted the *Preceptor* with a determination the aliens lacked. He found a spot directly between then shot at full thrust for it. One planetoid fired at them and missed. As it did, the radiation cannon beam struck squarely against the other armored planetoid.

"They're damaging each other now. Something's wrong with their computers," Chikako said. "They must be mistaking each other for us."

The vidscreen showed the cataclysmic explosion when one planetoid blew the other apart. Sarov took the opportunity to lay a barrage of missiles directly onto the rocky surface of the survivor. Seconds later, huge gouts of flame spat outward; he had scored a direct hit on a buried power plant.

"We are taking heavy fire from the planet's surface," he said, not taking the time to gloat over the *Preceptor*'s dual victory. "We can pinpoint and destroy, if we use the radiation cannon."

Norlin switched control of the captured alien weapon directly to Sarov's board. The tac officer immediately let the expert systems program take over to aim and fire. The power levels dropped drastically, dimming lights and causing Norlin's displays to flicker ominously.

"Barse!" he shouted. "What's wrong?"

"Nothing, Cap'n. It's the radiation cannon. It's sucking all our power."

"The switch? Isn't it working?"

"It couldn't do better. You're asking too much of the power plant. We don't use half this much power when we activate the shift engines."

Norlin saw the power indicators dropping dramatically as Sarov used the cannon as a continuous wave weapon. He didn't pulse it or give it a instant's rest. The deadly beam cut through the defensive net surrounding Kindar and blasted away huge sections of the planet's surface.

Just when Norlin began to worry about their own survival, Sarov stopped using the radiation cannon and switched back to missiles. Then he interspersed their AI-guided flight with the three forward lasartillery batteries. He had gone back to the radiation cannon for a final pass against the planet when Chikako barked, "Captain, listen to the message. The Kindarians are asking for a ceasefire. They want to surrender!"

"Trahnee! Listen in. Tell me what you think." Norlin shifted the audio to the vidscreen to allow her to evaluate the alien's message of surrender.

*Brutal vessels ravaging our world, we send you greetings and a desire for peace. Cease to destroy. We will negotiate. We will meet your terms for truce.*

"They are not to be trusted," warned Oloroun. "They fight too poorly and want only to dupe you."

"No, Oloroun, we've got them," Norlin said. "We beat them, and they're ready to quit." He hoped he was right, but the bear alien's words carried a ring of truth to them. The Kindarians showed no stomach for having their world destroyed, yet destroyed others with alacrity.

"Their most ruthless might be in their marauding fleet," Trahnee said, picking up on his hesitation. "Behind are left only those unable to fight."

Norlin checked the *Preceptor*'s damage before worrying more about the Kindarian message. They had sustained little impairment of their capabilities. A dozen other ships in his small fleet had not been so lucky—they were lifeless hulks. The remaining twelve ships could fight but poorly. The Kindarian radiation cannons had taken their toll.

He had no idea of the condition of the ships he had sent to decoy away the armored planetoids. That tactic had worked well enough—fully half the planetoids had turned from their defensive orbits and lumbered after the other part of his fleet.

"We're getting a laser com-link," said Chikako. "Two ships survived their scavenger hunt across the system. No word on how many enemy planetoids were destroyed. Not many, if any, from preliminary debris data."

"We'll negotiate with the Kindarians on-planet," Norlin decided. "Get the other ships back here as fast as you can. We'll need them to back up our claim."

"How can the surrender of their homeworld affect their Death Fleet?" asked Gowan Liottey. "They cannot know where their ships have gone. After Epsilon Eridani, they scattered."

"They might return home. If they do, they won't go out again."

Norlin frowned. Liottey's question bothered him. Destroying Kindar seemed less worthy a goal than it had before. He could do it. But why bother? It might not stop the Death Fleet already blasting its way across human-colonized space.

"They're sending a homing beacon signal," said Chikako. "Captain, we should determine the place for surrender. Have them come to us."

"I'm not landing," Norlin said decisively. "Have them pick one of their armored planetoids. We'll meet there."

"That's dangerous," Sarov said. "We—"

"We need to show them we're in charge. This ought to give them the idea we're not afraid of those satellites. Even if we are."

Norlin knew the Kindarians might win the battle through simple attrition. He had to present a strong face to them and bluff his way through, pretending to be the spearpoint of a far larger invading force.

Chikako worked for several minutes; Norlin didn't concern himself with the ebb and flow of the conversation. He worked with Liottey to contain the worst of the leakage from the hull and gas systems and start repair. Several of their main power conduits had been destroyed. It would take a significant amount of work in dry dock to fix the damage, but the *Preceptor* would be up for it after he obtained the peace treaty with the Kindarians.

"The planetoid showing the alternating green-and-yellow beacon is their flagship, Captain," reported Chikako. "They want to use it for the surrender."

Norlin looked around the cramped bridge and nodded. There wasn't room for the surrender to take place onboard. More than this, he didn't want the aliens to see the sorry condition of his ship and decide to continue the fight. He nodded briskly.

"Arrange it," he said.

"Pier, wait." Trahnee took his arm. "This isn't right. Oloroun is correct. They surrendered too easily."

"Too easily?" He swung around and flipped the zoom on the vidscreen. The destruction wrought on the planet's surface had been immense. Sarov's use of the radiation cannon had maximized annihilation. Where mountains had soared now bubbled seas of molten rock. Parts of ocean had boiled off. Cities had been leveled.

"Yes, Pier. Think about it. You make a single pass over their world and they quit? Does this sound like the same enemy that you've fought for so long? They aren't the type to simply give up after a few setbacks. Until we chained him to the deck plates, our prisoner tried every possible way to escape."

"You think it's a trap? It might be." He glanced at the vidscreen picture of the armored planetoid where the surrender was to be formalized. "They've stopped firing. We have our other two ships coming in to reinforce us. If they try any treachery, we will lay waste to their planet until nothing remains. There won't be a rock that sticks up more than ten centimeters above another. We will level their world, liquefy its very crust."

"Don't forget most of the destruction came from Sarov's use of the radiation cannon. The *Preceptor* is our only ship with it."

"They don't know that," Norlin said. "We have to risk this. If we keep fighting, we're all dead, and they win by attrition."

"Be careful." Trahnee put the full power of her genhanced talent into those two words. He felt but resisted the tug, knowing he didn't need such reinforcement of his basic nature.

Smiling gently, he touched her cheek.

"We'll be alright. A different party might have been left in charge of their planet. Perhaps these didn't approve of the Death Fleet policy."

Trahnee shook her head. Norlin had to admit the words rang hollow in his own ears.

He worked a few minutes at his command board before turning it over to Sarov.

"I will keep a close watch on the spidery bastards, Captain," the tac officer declared. "I do not often agree with *her*…" He said inclining his crewcut head in Trahnee's direction. "…but this time she is making sense. Something is not right."

Norlin stretched and left the bridge, the uneasiness gnawing at him. He had done what he could. The Kindarian representative had sued for peace. He had to oblige.

"Gowan, I want you to accompany me when we go over to the planetoid."

"Yes, sir," the first officer said. "I've been watching the prisoner. What do you make of his behavior?" Liottey flipped a switch and opened the circuit to the spider-like creature's cell.

Curled up, the Kindarian shivered as if he froze to death. All eight legs curled in at their ends, and his hands were tightly clenched. Norlin shifted the focus and tried to find the creature's eyes to look at them. He hid his face in the center of the morass of legs.

"He looks as if he's preparing to die," Norlin said.

"Cap'n," cut in Barse over his com-link, "we're jockeying for position at their hollowed-out asteroid now. Their docking facilities are open and waiting for us. Pretty landing beacon and all. Do you want me to shuttle you over?"

"Liottey and I will—"

The ship shuddered as the radiation cannon on the Kindarian's armored planetoid opened fire on them.

# Chapter Eighteen

cceleration slammed Norlin flat against a bulkhead. He struggled to get his hand to the com-link at his belt.

"Sarov, what's our status?" he shouted,

"Damned ship has a mind of its own," the tac officer growled. "I am trying to turn off the drive. We are heading into space at a tangent to the planet. Bearing is hard to calculate right now."

"I set the drive on auto to get us out if the Kindarians tried anything." Norlin explained. "What's the damage? How badly did they hurt us?"

"Bad, Cap'n," came Barse's appraisal. "The main lasartillery batteries are out. Power leads are fused. We've still got power to the radiation cannon, but the lasers are completely gone. I'm not sure about the missile tubes."

"Two lost," said Sarov. "We are almost helpless."

"What of the armored planetoid?"

"The other ships in orbit report it's exploded," said Chikako. "Get to the bridge as fast as possible—you aren't going to believe this. They're suiciding. All the armored planetoids are blowing up to take out our ships."

"Get on with repairing the lasartillery," he ordered Liottey. "And when you've got the RRUs on that, bring the prisoner to the bridge. I want Trahnee to question him about this."

"He can't know what they intended, Captain," Liottey said. He saw Norlin's dark expression, "I'll bring him to you shortly, sir, as soon as I can get him unwelded from the deck."

"Do it."

Norlin struggled to his feet. The high acceleration he had programmed into the navigational computer had taken him by surprise. He hadn't wanted Sarov, Trahnee and Oloroun to be right, but he had taken precautions, nevertheless. He had ordered the computer to launch the ship away from the source of danger as fast as possible. The computer had blasted them tangential to the planet when the planetoid opened fire on them.

The engines cut off as suddenly as they had started. Norlin dropped to one knee and caught himself before he banged his head. Working forward, he entered the control room.

Chikako's scalplock blazed with the com traffic. Sarov worked like a madman at his board. Trahnee had dropped into the command chair and slowly reviewed the damage reports, optimizing the RRUs being dispatched to repair essential systems. Oloroun stood beside the command chair, passing along his observations from the data on the ship's vidscreen.

"No immediate danger," she reported, leaving the chair to make room for Norlin. "The hull is intact, and we can breathe."

"I put Liottey onto repairing the lasartillery system. It doesn't look as if we'll get firepower back without major overhauling."

"They used the radiation cannon on us, then blew up their own station," Trahnee said. "Look at the vidscreen. They're trying to remove all our ships the same tactic."

Norlin frowned. This might be the aliens' best option—remove all the ships in a one-for-one trade and believe that no more of the ES fleet was on its way. They had called his bluff, but something still didn't seem right to him.

"They're robot units," he said, after considering the problem. "Those aren't driven by intelligent beings. The spider-creatures left robot armored planetoids. This is a robot's method for maximizing enemy destruction."

"Chances are good that you are right," said Sarov. "I cannot see any gain to the Kindarians exchanging such massive space forts plus a crew for a single ship."

Norlin worked to bring the *Preceptor* back under his control.

It took more than ten hours to return to orbit. By then, the two surviving ships he had split from the initial invasion force had joined the few still in orbit. He felt sick. The additional pair of ships almost doubled his force.

"Six ships," he moaned. "And none is in condition to fight."

"The Kindarian tactic worked well. What are we going to do now?" asked Oloroun.

"Suggestions?"

Norlin looked around the control room. Sarov frowned then said that he might have an answer to this call for tactics.

"Nuke the planet," the dour tactical officer suggested. "Lay down a steady barrage as the planet turns under us. We can destroy it with missiles in only one rotation."

"We can have the other ships use their lasartillery," said Norlin. "We don't have to join in."

"Cap'n, the radiation cannon is operational," Barse reported. "The lasartillery is out for the duration, as are five launch tubes."

"Three tubes and the cannon," he said. "Very well. Pass along my order, Sarov. Open bombardment of the planet. Fire at will, using any weapon capable of inflicting maximum destruction."

Trahnee gasped, but Oloroun took her hand and pulled her down to his level. The Prothasian spoke rapidly with her for several seconds. Whatever he said mollified her.

Norlin's pitifully few ships avoided the remaining armored planetoids in orbit around the enemy planet and turned their attention to the surface of the world. Less than four hours after the systematic destruction began, Chikako reported a second Kindarian message suing for peace.

"They're joking!" blurted Barse, hearing the message. "They think we'll fall for their trick a second time?"

"I don't know what they think. That's the problem," said Norlin. He touched the com-link and got his first officer on a private circuit. "Gowan, have you gotten far enough on the repair work to escort our prisoner to the bridge?"

"I can, Captain," said Liottey. "Work is going slowly. I hate to say it, but Barse is right about the major components of the weapons system. They'll have to be ripped out in dry dock and replaced. Field repair isn't going to be good enough."

"Do what you can. And get the prisoner here. I need to know if the suicide explosion was strictly robotic or if this is standard policy and they cannot surrender. It looked like treachery on their part, but we might have done something to violate the truce in their eyes. I don't want a repeat if there is any chance of getting them to surrender."

Norlin waited impatiently as Liottey brought the spider-like being into the control room. The first officer stood with his hand on the butt of his laser pistol, but Trahnee's voice proved a more effective binding than any chains.

"You will sit and not move," she ordered. The genhanced woman sweated profusely as she worked with the Kindarian. "Only truth will be spoken. Do you understand?"

"There is truth in this. Understanding is mine."

"Why did your people ask for a ceasefire and then attack us?"

"Chance prevails," the prisoner said. He curled six of his legs around his hard thorax and turned into a fuzzy ball.

"Explain this," urged Trahnee.

Norlin shivered with the vibrant power in the words. From the corner of his eye, he saw Liottey's lips quivering. Even standing several meters away, Trahnee affected him, too, and the first officer had to fight her implacable order.

"Chance rules all," the Kindarian said. A huge compound eye peered out of the tangle of legs at Trahnee. "They thought to win. Odds rode with them. The odds changed. They try to maximize win. How else can you run your affairs?"

"Let me get this straight," pressed Norlin. "Probability said a sneak attack would succeed, so they tried it. Now that the attack failed, probability says we can win, so your people will surrender?"

The prisoner's head wobbled from side to side in a gesture Norlin interpreted as meaning assent.

"What do the rest of you think?" He directed his question to the entire crew.

"We hit them severely this time. They might not be able to continue their attack from planetside," said Sarov. "There is no question that they are hurting more now than before. The loss of so many of their planetoids hinders their defense, too."

"They've got a dozen armored planetoids returning—the ones we decoyed away aren't destroyed," Chikako reminded him. "I've talked with the other com officers. The decoy fleet lost three ships, but none of the planetoids was destroyed. They may be slow, but they'll get back here sometime soon."

"They will surrender this time," Trahnee said after thinking it over.

"I agree, Cap'n. We hit 'em too hard not to call it quits," said Barse. His engineer's response startled him. She was usually bloodthirsty and ready to fight. "I say we take their surrender at face value."

"Gowan? You've been closer to the prisoner than any of us. What do you think?"

"They have truly surrendered this time. Accept it."

Norlin nodded. A race ruled by the laws of probability could be defeated by shifting the odds. He had done that. He should have known that surrender before had come too easily. This time the Empire Service fleet had inflicted serious damage to the planet's surface. Wherever the Kindarian headquarters was—they had been unable to pinpoint it—he guessed the beings there were the only ones still alive on-planet.

"We'll try to get their agreement to stop," Norlin decided. "But this time we call the shots completely. They have to stop the return of their armored planetoids before we talk. Pass that along to them."

Chikako had barely transmitted the demand when she ripped off part of the wiring going through her scalplock. Glassy-eyed, she said, "They blew up all their planetoids."

"Confirmed," said Sarov.

Norlin saw the message not only on his two officers' boards but also from his other ships circling the planet. He settled down. Whatever tricks the Kindarians had tried before, they were helpless now. The odds against them having a weapon more powerful than their armored, hollowed-out asteroids were great. If such a weapon existed, they would have used it.

"Send an envoy to my ship. A shuttle will land for your ambassador," he told the Kindarians. "Signal where the shuttle is to land."

"Captain, let them come up in their own shuttle," suggested Chikako, still dazed from the overload on her com circuits.

"We'll know what's in the ship if we send one of ours," he said. "I don't want to find a nuke locked up in the landing bay—or some other unpleasant surprise."

"I'll go, Cap'n," volunteered Barse.

"Liottey will take the shuttle down. He's had more experience with them."

"I can speak a little of their language," came the surprising answer from the first officer. "I'm terrible at it—I can't repeat the clicks and whistles they use for nouns and adjectives—but I'm good at verbs."

"Go," ordered Norlin. "And get the spiders' ambassador back here fast. I want an end to this." When Liottey had gone, taking their prisoner back to his cell, Norlin said to Trahnee, "I need you to be our main negotiator. Get a promise to cease and desist with attacks on all our colonies."

"We'll have to find out the power status of their ambassador. He might be a minor functionary unable to recall the Death Fleet."

"Recalling them might be beyond anyone's authority on this world."

Norlin leaned back and stared at the vidscreen display of Kindar. Something worried him about the planet's appearance. For a world that had launched thousands of ships in the alien death fleet, it hardly seemed...enough.

✳ ✳ ✳

He was still deep in through when Liottey returned two hours later with the solitary ambassador from the planet. Norlin swung around and stared at the spider-like being. History was being made—and it didn't seem that way. He wondered if the lack of puissance meant he had again guessed wrong about the Kindarians and their intentions.

"For you, master of this fleet, I bring only warm greetings and liquid surrender," the Kindarian ambassador said. He performed a weird dance, all eight limbs moving in a complex pattern. Norlin glanced at Liottey, who shook his head. The first officer had no idea what this ceremony meant.

Trahnee said, "It's a ritual surrender. Note how the Kindarian keeps his hands open to show there aren't any hidden weapons. There's more to it, I suspect, but I need much more information on them to tell you what else is being said."

"We accept the unconditional surrender of the Kindar race," Norlin said. "On behalf of Emperor Arian and the Empire Service, I applaud you for your good sense in protecting your homeworld."

He didn't need Trahnee's sharp grip on his arm or Oloroun's hiss to know that he had said something wrong. The Kindarian ambassador stopped his bizarre dance and simply stared at him, huge black compound eyes unreadable.

"Why do you stop your dance of surrender?" demanded Trahnee. The full power of her genhanced talent went into that question. The Kindarian trembled under its sonic force.

"You think I represent my race? I cannot give you the surrender of all my people."

"What of the Death Fleet?"

"The Force of Liberation From Planetary Shackles of Want and Need?" the spider-like creature asked. "They are independent. They travel beyond my capacity to ever know. They return one day with enough to maintain us."

"You have no contact with your Force of Liberation?" asked Norlin.

"They were sent forth to contend with your viciousness. You attack aliens not of your kind."

"Oloroun," called Trahnee. "He is our friend and ally." She put her hand on the small Prothasian's shoulder. "We do not have a good record of relations with other races, but you made no effort to contact us. Your Death Fleet destroyed and raped, then went on to another world and repeated it. This is an act of war."

The Kindarian shrugged.

"We compute probabilities. In that lies our hope of survival against you. Communication with other races and our own comprehensive information analysis condemned you. Our Force of Liberation had no choice."

Norlin pressed the point that had startled him.

"You are not able to give us the total surrender of Kindar? You don't speak for everyone on-planet?"

"I speak for everyone on this world," the Kindarian said.

Trahnee asked the question that turned Norlin's guts cold.

"Isn't this planet your homeworld? Isn't this Kindar?"

The Kindarian danced about and then hunkered down on the deck. If a spider could laugh, Norlin thought this one was having a great laugh at their expense.

"This miserable world is not the world of our home. It is not Kindar."

Norlin sagged. Once again they had fought the enemy only to find that complete victory eluded them. He had sustained great losses conquering a world that wasn't Kindar.

# Chapter Nineteen

I t's not Kindar," Norlin said tiredly. "We've defeated them, and it's the wrong damned world!"

"We still have ships able to fight," said Sarov. "We can scavenge the destroyed ships, what is left of them, and borrow parts from the others to get a couple into fighting trim."

"No, we can't," Norlin said. "The *Preceptor* is in better shape than most. Barse, tell him what you told me."

"He knows, Cap'n. We all know. We've got two missile tubes that might not blow up on us. No lasartillery. The radiation cannon is in good condition, and the power plant can feed it."

"The fleet has been destroyed as a fighting force," he said. "We can't meet the defense likely to surround their homeworld and hope to bring them to the negotiating table. We took too heavy losses getting this far into the Black Nebula."

"Are you sure, Pier?" asked Trahnee. "Consider the nature of the worlds we've seen. Look at this one. The ambassador is one of only five hundred on the entire planet."

"Still living," grumbled Norlin. "How many were there before we raked the planet with nukes and our radiation cannon?"

"Not many more," piped up Oloroun. "I have spoken at length with ambassador of the spider things." The Prothasian jumped up and squatted on the arm of Norlin's command chair. "No more than ten times this were on this world."

"Five thousand? That's not even a well-staffed observation outpost, much less a colony world," protested Norlin. "Why did they guard it so heavily if that few lived on the surface?"

"You spoke truly," Oloroun reminded him, "when you mentioned the robotic nature of their defense. They relied much on machines, not living beings. This is the brilliance of your fine victory. The genhanced humans fought with genius, the machines fought with inferior programs."

"What are you saying?" asked Norlin.

"We are running it through our computer now," said Sarov. "The fuzz-face might have hit on the answer. The worst may be behind us. Kindar might not be as hard to take as we thought when we entered the nebula."

"It's a long way to come to find we can't affect the Death Fleet," said Norlin. He looked over at Sarov and Chikako when they bent over their boards. He moved Oloroun to one side and displayed their results on the vidscreen.

He blinked when he saw the most probable answer to the questions Sarov and Chikako had asked.

"Their homeworld might not be defended at all? That's utterly preposterous," he said.

"We cannot know for sure," admitted Sarov. "We can only use the data collected and analyze it to the best of our ability. As you can see, two or three ships might be able to claim Kindar for the empire. The *Preceptor* might, as damaged as we are."

"Another trap," decided Norlin. "They're masters of probability. It rules their lives. They've laid out this for us to use as they would—It must be a trap. You can't be right."

Sarov shrugged his huge shoulders.

"I have been wrong before. This feels right, though." The tac officer went back to working on esoteric problems not making their way to the vidscreen.

"We go on," Norlin decided. "Sarov might be right—or I might be. The only way to find out is to go to Kindar and see. We'll need to have message packets ready to launch back to Earth with complete details." He had no confidence that Tidzio would ever tell the emperor what was contained in such messages, but at least he would have done all he could to alert the empire.

He went to his controls and added several more destinations for message packets, all to colony worlds.

"The ambassador spoke truthfully of his homeworld's location," Trahnee assured him. "I only wish I could have gotten more from him. There is a curious blockage when he speaks of it."

"He has never seen it," said Oloroun. "Listen and you will know. He worships it. His veneration knows no bounds, but he has never seen it. All his life, he has lived on this world."

"You might be right, Oloroun." Trahnee frowned as she considered the ramifications of this.

Norlin saw that the time had passed for careful consideration. Action was needed, even if he had bad feelings about shifting into a trap. He had to admit Sarov might be right—the man had more experience than he did, and he *was* the tactical expert.

"Pass these orders along, Chikako." He settled into his command chair and stared at the vidscreen. "Leave the most damaged ships in orbit with orders to nuke this planet to a radioactive cinder at the first sign of resistance. The other three ships will shift for Kindar with us in one hour."

Pier Norlin sank down farther in the chair, unable to shake off the feeling he had just signed the death order for the last of his command.

✳ ✳ ✳

"Battle stations, all hands to battle stations!" barked Norlin. The *Preceptor* had shifted into normal space in the center of the Kindarian's home solar system. He didn't want anyone taken by surprise by another instant attack.

"Picking up missiles," said Chikako. "Slow and not very large. Do you confirm that they are missiles?"

"No," said Sarov. "Those are mines. Ancient, if my readings are accurate. We can sweep them out of our path if they try to attach and be inside their defensive perimeter in minutes."

"Do it," ordered Norlin.

He frowned as he saw how archaic those defensive mines were. Such implements had been discarded on Earth five hundred years earlier. Why did a culture capable of launching the Death Fleet rely on such primitive methods for defending its homeworld?

"There's Kindar," said Trahnee, moving to increase the magnification on the vidscreen. The dust inside the nebula obscured the view a little, but Chikako had done well in correcting for the veiling particles.

Norlin increased the magnification a hundredfold and simply stared at the sight.

"All ships, stand down from battle stations," he said.

He moved the cruiser forward slowly, letting Sarov pluck out the mines with deft touches of his own missiles, and put the ship into orbit around Kindar. Only after two complete orbits did he relax. This wasn't a trap. It wasn't a clever alien ploy to lure his fleet to its destruction.

It was a completely spent world, ruined beyond redemption.

"Any life readings?" he asked Chikako.

"None. No power leakage, no indications of civilization at all—except for that single building."

The vidscreen shimmered and focused on the top of a mountain that had been leveled to form a ten-square-kilometer plain. Indications of a small building in the center gave them the only hint that life had ever existed on this world.

"This is even worse than the other worlds," said Trahnee.

"Bad air," agreed Oloroun, staring at Norlin's readouts. "Choke to death on air. Acid in air, in water, everywhere."

"It is more than that. The minerals have been mined out. I have evidence now of mines sunk more than twenty kilometers into the mantle. They stripped everything usable. No petroleum products. Those wind erosion channels were used for garbage dumps—but it was a long time ago," said Sarov.

"No life readings," Norlin repeated over and over. "Is this *really* their homeworld?"

"Get prisoner here. Ask him your fine question," suggested Oloroun.

Norlin buzzed for Liottey to bring the prisoner to the bridge. When the Kindarian saw the single building centered on the vidscreen, he fell to the deck. His eight limbs began a complicated weaving.

"Another communication or ritual dance," suggested Trahnee. To the Kindarian, she said, "Tell us of this building. What are we looking at?"

"The Fountain of Spacefaring," he said with more reverence than he had ever shown before. "It is the most sacred shrine of my race."

"You wouldn't want us to nuke it?" asked Norlin.

The spider-like creature went berserk. Two legs knocked Liottey back. Another struck Oloroun and disabled him. The Kindarian shot forward, hands reaching for Norlin's throat. Two pale laser beams winked on, one from Sarov's sidearm and the other from Chikako Miza's. Even slicing off all the legs on one side of the Kindarian's body did not keep him from grabbing Norlin.

Norlin broke the grip and slid from his chair to better fight the violent creature. Sarov finished with a bolt to the Kindarian's thorax. Even then, the being thrashed and tried to use his talons on Norlin.

"I've seen powerful responses before, but nothing like that."

"Captain," cried Liottey, "I'm sorry. He took me by surprise. He's been so docile…"

"It's all right. We found out what he thinks of this place, this Fountain of Spacefaring."

"We could have saved him," mourned Trahnee. "He could have been useful."

"Good work, Sarov, Miza," congratulated Norlin, ignoring her. He turned back to the vidscreen and stared at it.

"What is for us on this world?" asked Oloroun. "We see nothing of them. We bring nothing to stop them from plundering of your colonies."

"This place holds a special meaning for the Kindarians," Norlin said. "You saw how our prisoner reacted." He wrinkled his nose as the robots cleaned the decks and removed the corpse. He had no love for the Kindarian, not after all he and his kind had done to his worlds.

"They've destroyed their own world," said Chikako. "They've laid waste to it as surely as they've done on any of our worlds. Why?"

"They didn't know any better. They must have reached a stage in their civilization that required materials—and they just took them. They paid no attention to what happened around them," suggested Trahnee.

"That's incredible," admitted Norlin. "It looks as if you are right, though. This world is depleted. They've sucked everything from it they can and left behind only the industrial wastes. When they ran out of the stuff keeping them alive, they moved on to other worlds and duplicated their profligacy."

"Only the building remains. Do you want me to nuke it?" asked Sarov.

"I want to explore it before you do," said Norlin. "Any clue to the Kindarian mentality is vital if we are to stop them permanently."

"I'll drop a shuttle full of robots to flutter around and send back pretty pictures," said Barse.

A few minutes later, Norlin felt the ship shudder as the shuttle launched. Within twenty minutes, the vidscreen popped into a poor imitation of life in gray-and-brown tints. The shuttle had landed in front of the Kindarian relic and disgorged the small flying robots equipped with vidcameras.

"Get good pictures," urged Trahnee. "I want to study them later."

He looked at her. She had shown increasing interest in the Kindarian culture—and the spider-like creatures themselves—since coming aboard. He saw how it would aid the empire to have an anthropologist or xeno-sociologist as part of the crew. Then he felt hollow inside. He sought any reason possible to keep her in his crew when he would not have a command once they returned to Earth.

Norlin felt a pang—he knew the answer to that dilemma. Don't return to Earth.

"Full computer workup on the data," he ordered. He found himself increasingly curious about the aliens, too. Hatred still burned in him for what their Death Fleets had done, but he now had a chance to view their most private nature.

"We're trying to translate the markings now," Chikako said. "We have a few hints on what they mean, but it'll take some time. I'm going on the assumption that the main lettering spells out Fountain of Spacefaring."

Norlin stared at the once-ornate stone building. The facade had long since been eroded by wind and pockmarked from acid rain. Low steps marched up to four pillared entries, each without a door. He followed the vid from the central robot as it flittered up and into the building. The roof had miraculously survived. Sunlight filtered in, blood-red and distorted from the atmospheric pollution, and bathed a simple altar.

"There's only the one large room. It's a religious structure. A church," said Chikako. "No, not that. It has something to do with what they believe, but it's not got anything to do with a deity."

"A philosophy," ventured Trahnee. "This is the heart of their philosophy. They took everything they could from their homeworld and simply abandoned it—except for this single building."

"The Fountain of Spacefaring," said Norlin. "This is a monument to honor their departure from Kindar. They wasted their own world and went on to do it to every other world they found."

"Their colony world we just left must be about all that is left in the Black Nebula," said Sarov. "There's not enough here to support even a small city."

"The ambassador thought his fleet would return with supplies. They went out to plunder and bring back the spoils to their colonies in the nebula?" Norlin saw the twisted sense this made for the aliens.

"They all left—or died," said Trahnee. "The Death Fleet constitutes their entire race. Everyone, except the very few left behind, is with the Death Fleet."

"We destroy their fleet, and we destroy the Kindarians," said Sarov. "We have what we came for, Captain. We have got the way to fight them to extinction."

"Sarov's right, Cap'n," said Barse. "We know that once the Death Fleet is eliminated, all the Kindarians are, too."

Norlin didn't feel vindicated. All they said was true, but he felt there should be more.

"Translation coming through on the writing," said Chikako. "The computers are working...working...working...there!"

Norlin looked at the vidscreen and saw the rune-like characters superimposed with translation.

"Four Death Fleets," he said. "We've sent one fleet running and probably done enough damage on the rest to account for another. That leaves half their total population to contend with."

The translation ran on, giving a history of the Kindarians, a frightening story of misuse of their planetary resources and the plundering of nearby worlds. Not once had they considered altering their lifestyle as they raped their way through the sparse newly formed worlds of the Black Nebula. The four Death Fleets had not been readied to bring back needed materiel to those left in the Black Nebula; they had been a continuation of policies mired in the ancient dawn of Kindarian prehistory.

"They started as vandals, and they're going to end that way," said Norlin. "They never learned to live with their world. Look at that translation. They say all other races oppose them. They know damned little or nothing about us. They use the same excuse for any inhabited world. If we have material they want, they take it."

"It fit," Oloroun said in a low voice. "They did not know you, yet it fit too well."

"We can eradicate them," said Chikako. "Here is the initial trajectory for each of their fleets. We demolished number three. Two is mostly ruined, from previous encounters with Admiral Bendo and other worlds."

"And the other two," said Trahnee, "are not even near human—colonized space. They might have found new worlds to colonize with the intention of spawning even more Death Fleets to spread in other directions."

"Lies," said Oloroun, "told to you are magnified. They did not try to contact you because of your treatment of us. They despoil because it is their way."

"I'm afraid you're right," said Norlin. "We've got a job ahead of us that might be even harder than defeating the remaining Kindarians. We've got to forge a bond of trust between Prothasian and human—and try to reach the other aliens, too."

"They reject you for all time," Oloroun said firmly. "I do not blame them. Emperor Arian's treatment of us is as bad as Death Fleet of your worlds."

"We can change. I don't think the Kindarians can," he replied. "It's part of their genetic makeup."

"Genes are destiny," Trahnee said, as if repeating a litany.

Norlin looked at her in surprise. The future might be even bleaker than he thought if all the genhanced held that as their credo. From what he had seen in the emperor's court, they did.

"We've got complete photos of everything in their Fountain of Spacefaring," said Chikako. "An exterior view shows how it used to have a fluted roof like a fountain spewing out all it held. What do we do now?"

"Record it when we blow the damned place to hell, where it belongs," said Norlin.

"A moment, please," said Oloroun. "I want not to stop you with this act of violence. May I add to the moment's significance?" The Prothasian held out the millennia-old samurai sword.

At first, Norlin didn't understand what Oloroun suggested. Then, understanding began to grow when he saw the importance of making the gesture. A smile crossed his lips as he took the blade.

"Thank you for the suggestion, Oloroun. Barse, get a robot to take this down and place it on the Kindarian altar. *Then* blow the hell out of the place."

Oloroun bobbed his furred head up and down in agreement with Norlin's symbolic breaking of old human ways and the acts of the empire.

✳ ✳ ✳

Norlin waited until the small tracked robot had deposited the sword in the center of the alien altar. He touched a single toggle on his board, giving Sarov permission to proceed. The tactical officer responded immediately. Nuclear-warhead-tipped missiles dropped from orbit and blew the alien building to atoms.

They had come so far, and this was all the revenge Norlin—or anyone else—was likely to get. It didn't seem enough, not for worlds destroyed—or even for a single life that had been lost. But it would have to do.

# Chapter Twenty

We've won," Pier Norlin said without any enthusiasm. Static crackled over the com-link between the surviving ships in the Empire Service's fleet. "The Kindarians are a known factor now. We know what it will take to defeat them totally. We might even have an edge on them."

He went on to explain how the destruction of their Fountain of Spacefaring might turn the tide in any future battles. The shrine had been their only link to the depleted planet of their origin. Destroyed, it might demoralize them.

Norlin paused and let the import of all he'd said sink in. A handful of ships would return to empire-controlled space; the ships orbiting the Kindarian colony world had been stripped to make those returning as spaceworthy as possible. Even then, he worried that many of them would not be able to survive the long shift back to human-colonized space. More than five thousand light-years was a difficult shift, even with fully functional equipment.

He glanced at the displays showing how Liottey and Barse worked with their robot teams to bring the *Preceptor* back to minimal shift standards. Their firepower was gone, except for the radiation cannon. He was hesitant to order the alien equipment dismantled, even though they had to do it eventually to find out the secrets of the Kindarian super-weapon. He wanted to return to empire-controlled space with some offensive capability.

Emperor Arian would have placed a reward on the head of "Admiral" Norlin. A return to Earth was as out of the question for him as it was for Trahnee and Oloroun.

He looked at the small, furred alien and saw a better future in the Prothasian. Oloroun had aided them to the best of his ability in their fight against the Kindarians and the emperor. He had shown himself to be a true friend and worthy of their assistance.

Norlin would give it. They would return Oloroun to his world and try to forge bonds of trust and trade between Protha and the human-settled colonies. He wouldn't bother trying to negotiate for the empire. The time had come to break free of imperial rule. The genhanced officers might think differently, but he would leave that choice for them.

"I have given each navigational officer a timetable for departure from the Black Nebula and arrival at the colony world of Newcombe. If any ship is lost, we will have some idea about shift direction. A search can be mounted along that geodesic line." He believed that a search might be started, but practically, any ship lost during shift was lost for all time.

"Admiral Norlin," came a faint voice, "what do we do after we enter the Newcombe system?"

"That is up to you. I recommend each of you follow your conscience." He took a deep breath. "I, however, am not returning to Earth—or the Empire Service."

"Tidzio would have a price on your head, wouldn't he?" came the question.

"Undoubtedly. Those genhanced officers in your rank—and that is a majority—are free to do as they please. Any attempt to coerce me or the crew of the *Preceptor* to return to Earth will be met with all the power at my command."

"Sir, you misunderstand," came the voice. "We wish to follow you. I polled the officers. Those who have served under you agree that the strongest should rule. You are the strongest. Return with us to Earth, and we will place you on the Crystal Throne!"

Norlin smiled. He looked at Trahnee, thinking she might take them up on the offer. He saw her expression and knew she had found other interests. Oloroun fascinated her. She had formed a bond of friendship with the small alien that had replaced her desire to rule from the Crystal Throne.

"We have no desire to do that. I want only to find a frontier world and settle there. My skills are needed to protect the frontier from other segments of the Death Fleet—and from future empire intrusion."

"You don't want to rule?" The officer's voice reflected his shock and surprise.

"I want only to live peacefully. I was raised on the frontier and want to defend it. The Kindarians still threaten, though not as they once did. I have no need to tell you that the fringe worlds are slowly drifting away from the sphere of imperial rule. The day isn't far off when Earth will be left with a hollow empire, if it hasn't come to that already."

Norlin settled in his chair and let the chatter between the ships continue for several minutes. He had done what he had set out to do. Even though he had not personally defeated the Kindarians, he had gained valuable information that would aid others in destroying the Death Fleet, should it appear in colonial skies.

An even greater gift to mankind might be a treaty between the Prothasians and the colony worlds. They shared mutual enemies, both Kindarian and human. They could share much more than this, given the opportunity.

"Admiral Norlin—"

"I am resigning my Empire Service commission," Norlin cut in. "I am captain of the *Preceptor* and nothing more." He did not wish to point out that he had technically given cause for the other ships to turn on him—mutiny.

"Admiral Norlin," the officer pressed, "are there colony worlds where a genhanced officer can relocate without prejudice?"

"What?"

"Few among us want to return to Earth. Very few."

Norlin glanced at Chikako. She held up her left hand and flashed four fingers. Four out of forty officers desired a return to Empire Service.

"The remainder of you want to do what? You are guilty of mutiny and treason against the empire if you join the *Preceptor*—and me."

"We know. Not all genhanced are insane, as you believe, although among those remaining loyal to the emperor we think this is so now. We want to join those who live along the frontier." He laughed jovially. "That's where we're likely to find the most excitement!"

Norlin studied his board and saw that the computer instructions for departure had been received and approved by each ship, even those intending to return to Earth after reaching Newcombe. He wondered how many would change their minds about this desertion during the long shift back to human-colonized space.

He glanced around the control room and knew none of his officers would. They had discussed the future, and all wanted what he did. Oloroun held up small furred hands and clutched them together in a sign of victory. Norlin returned the gesture.

A good start.

"All ships," Norlin commanded, "prepare to shift…home."

END

# About the Author

**ROBERT E. VARDEMAN** is the author of nearly two hundred novels spanning many genres, but his favorites have always been science fiction and fantasy. He has served as vice-president of the Science Fiction Writers of America (SFWA) and also edited the organization's *Forum*. He is a member of the Western Writers of America (WWA) and the International Association of Media Tie-in Writers (IAMTW), serving as a judge for that organization's 2007 Scribe Award, and is also a member since its inception in 1979 of the informal group First Fridays, founded by mystery writer Tony Hillerman. For the past five years, he has worked on the editorial staff of four fantasy football magazines and is co-editor with Joan Saberhagen on the Baen Books anthology *Mask of the Sun: Golden Reflections*.

As a member of the Coalition for Excellence in Science Education, Vardeman served as consultant to the New Mexico State textbook advisory board in 2003.

# About the Artists

**BRAD W. FOSTER** is an illustrator, cartoonist, writer, publisher, and whatever other labels he can use to get him through the door. He's won the Fan Artist Hugo a few times, picked up a Chesley Award and turned a bit of self-publishing started more than twenty-five years ago into the Jabberwocky Graphix publishing empire. (Total number of employees: 2.)

His strange drawings and cartoons have appeared in more than two thousand publications, half of those science fiction fanzines, where he draws just for the fun of it. On a more professional level, he has worked as an illustrator for various genre magazines and publishers, including *Amazing Stories* and *Dragon*. In comics, he had his own series some years back, *The Mechthings*, and he even got to play with the "big boys" for a few years as the official "Big Background Artist" of Image Comic's *Shadowhawk*.

His intricate pen-and-ink work has appeared in places as varied as *Cat Fancy*, *Cavalier*, and *Highlights for Children*, *Space & Time* and *Talebones*, and in illustrations for the first of Carole Nelson Douglas's Cozy Noir Press books featuring Midnight Louie.

**TAMIAN WOOD** is currently based in sunny South Florida. Using art, photography, typography and digital collage techniques, she creates book covers that appeal to the eye and the mind, to entice the book browser to become a book reader. She holds degrees in computer science and graphic design and is a proud member of Phi Theta Kappa National Honour Society.

Made in the USA
Middletown, DE
22 October 2023

41270080R00123